P9-APE-289

THE
UNIVERSITY OF WINNIPEG
PORTAGE & BALMORAL
WINNIPEG, MAN.   R3B 2E9
CANADA

THE
EDINBURGH
STORIES

PR
4621
·E3
1981

THE EDINBURGH STORIES

of

Arthur Conan Doyle

POLYGON BOOKS

Cover by
JAMES HUTCHESON

ISBN 0 904919 49 8

Typeset in Bembo by
EDINBURGH UNIVERSITY STUDENT PUBLICATIONS BOARD

Reproduced from copy supplied,
printed and bound in Great Britain by
BILLING & SON LIMITED,
Guildford, London, Oxford, Worcester.

Published in 1981 by
E.U.S.P.B.,
1 Buccleuch Place, Edinburgh, EH8 9LW.

To

DAME JEAN CONAN DOYLE

CONTENTS

INTRODUCTION

ARTHUR CONAN DOYLE is a paradoxical figure among Edinburgh writers. Although almost all of the last fifty years of his life were spent in England, he took trouble to retain his Scottish accent, his wit and humour had a distinctively Scottish dry, analytical quality, he thronged his pages with memorable characters deriving in part from the Edinburgh intelligentsia and his vivid depiction of urban scenes owed far more initially to his birthplace than to the cities — notably London — in which they were nominally located. Yet posterity has hitherto granted little of this. His most recent biographer, the brilliant historian of the detective-story Julian Symons, tells us "he took away little from Edinburgh except his degree" and Trevor Royle's charming and erudite literary history of Edinburgh, *Precipitous City*, largely concurs.

But formative years were particularly critical in the case of so impressionable a creative writer distinguished for a phenomenally retentive memory, and the legacy of his Edinburgh experiences from birth in 1859 to departure in 1881 was a powerful one, although the two most substantial works with an Edinburgh location, the short story "John Barrington Cowles" and the short novel *The Parasite*, have been lost to sight for many years. The former survived for some time in the successive reprints of the author's early anthology *The Captain of the 'Polestar'* but was not brought into his later collections of his works; the latter, published as a single work, had several printings between 1894 and 1897 and then went out of print, and what stood most strongly against the reprinting of both stories was their length. The Sherlock Holmes short stories moved Conan Doyle from his often somewhat sprawling narratives of the 1880s to splendidly economic use of space in the 1890s and thereafter. He had, in fact, made himself the model for the multitude of professional short story writers who sprang into activity after his success in the *Strand* and poured out their offerings in its pages and those of its rivals to the time of his death.

The two stories fully merit survival. "Cowles" is certainly the work of a young author still in pursuit of a style, and while executed with remarkable power, occasionally shows a looseness in sentence-structure contrasting with the music and precision of his short-story writing from 1891 onward; but the admirers of Sherlock Holmes will find in it something of the same blend of scientifically presented evidence heightening the judicious anticipation and ultimate horrific climax of a plot all too worthy of Scottish literary traditions of fear and darkness. The Edinburgh setting, largely muted in *The Parasite* by reason of its special narrative form, plays a major part in the retrospection of "Cowles". A minor detail — having John Barrington Cowles win an actual and still existing prize in the Edinburgh medical school — reminds us at once both of those touches of personal humour with which Conan Doyle would surreptitiously introduce phenomena of his own experience into his fiction, and of the underlying tone of realism which has wooed so many enthusiasts into obsessions with Holmes, Watson and their adventures as creatures of fact.

The Parasite by contrast is the work of a mature writer of great technical skill. The narrator of "Cowles", benevolent but not particularly distinctive, has given way to a self-portrait of the protagonist worked out with the power for first-person narration which Doyle had by now shown in the creation of Watson. The use of the professor's day-to-day notes on the events at once conveys the mind of a scientific enquirer becoming gradually overwhelmed by his investigations, with dual effect both for character-depiction and for structural development. It is evident that Doyle had "Cowles" in mind in writing *The Parasite*. The mind-control episode in "Cowles", deeply arresting but rapidly disposed of, forms the basis for the entire plot of *The Parasite* and thus exemplifies what a remarkable craftsman could do in reworking ideas of which he had earlier made insufficient use. Above all else, Conan Doyle was a supreme master of literary economics. Another example of such reconsideration is the transformation of the conventional concept of a supremely attractive if diabolic beauty in "Cowles" to an essentially repulsive but even more dangerously destructive woman in *The Parasite*.

Conan Doyle rejected the crude acceptance of Roman Catholic doctrine, with all of its certainties, which his school training had sought to inculcate, but he also remained doubtful about the equal self-assurance of scientific scepticism as transmitted by the

Edinburgh University medical school. His life, both literary and spiritual, constantly reflected a mental conflict between science and the supernatural. Ultimately, Doyle was to find resolution of his long internal conflict in the spiritualistic faith, and to express the victory of spirit over science in the conquest of Professor Challenger, but a finer artistic expression of that resolution is to be found in the passages where the scientific Holmes acknowledges his belief in the spirit. This resolution lay far in the future during the writing of *The Parasite*, and part of the novel's strength is its revelation of the terrible vulnerability of seemingly all-conquering science. It is worth stressing that Doyle, conscious of his own Celtic antecedents, is also playing skilfully with the question of whether what is at stake is science or magic: as modern historians of science have testified, the two were decidedly allied, sometimes in the single persons of their medieval practitioners.

Location plays an interestingly contrasting role in another respect. The care of usage of local references in "Cowles" is in part intended to offset the plot, which could be located anywhere: Cowles might have met his fate whatever his city and profession, and the final scenes on the island are intended to imply just such a removal from normal social life. (They also offer a fascinating anticipation of the last great scene in "The Final Problem", where Watson calls into the deep from the cliff for the presumably dead Holmes, to hear a strange half-human response much as Armitage does for Cowles: again, the evidence of the growth of professional literary skill in the interval between composition of the two stories is highly suggestive.) In *The Parasite* the greater tension of the story is achieved by the disruption of Edinburgh social and academic life by the enchantment. The fate of Professor Gilroy affects this reader much more than that of Cowles, because the surroundings and circumstances come so much closer to the lives of reader and writer. Hesketh Pearson's *Conan Doyle* saw something of the strength of *The Parasite* but weakened itself by its own facetiousness, the English Pearson finding it ludicrous that Gilroy could be suspended from his chair for talking nonsense in lectures. But Doyle was thinking of his Edinburgh, where lectures were strictly linked to students' fees and were absolutely pre-eminent in the university system, having nothing of the comforts of the Oxbridge tutorials about them.

The sexual implications of both stories are notable, but they require rather more conservative analysis than Mr Charles Higham has offered in the biography where he so rightly seeks to rescue them from their obscurity. Conan Doyle's medical research for his doctorate was concerned with the effects of syphilis, and indeed some of his medical fiction, such as "The Third Generation" and "A Medical Document", introduces the theme in highly dramatic form. Given the readiness to label him a typical Victorian it is important to stress here, as elsewhere, he was in fact seeking to open up far more realistic dimensions to fiction. Moreover, as a medical student, he knew far more about sexual impulses and their possible consequences than most writers, and believed their discussion to be natural and necessary. "Cowles", composed at the time when he was finishing his doctoral thesis, is in part a metaphor for syphilis: human destruction by love for an instrument of murderous contagion. The metaphor is also present in *The Parasite*, but by making the destruction mental rather than physical it is strengthened, while retaining the medical basis that syphilis and its effects also destroy the mind. Lord Randolph Churchill was presenting a tragic proof of the fact in the House of Commons during these very years.

The diabolical women themselves, however, reflect a different aspect of Doyle. He was a believer in "the new woman" in many respects: the great creative period which produced *The Parasite* also included two very powerful statements for the rights of women in professional life, "The Doctors of Hoyland" and *Beyond the City*. In our two stories the women are evil, and women in Doyle's fiction are normally forces for good, if at times ambiguous and frustrated in that work. Doyle believed in the superiority of women, very largely because of his overwhelming admiration for his own mother, who kept a struggling family together despite his father's alcoholism and inability to take responsibility. These two stories show a female superiority turned to evil consequences, but the testament to that superiority is still there. Elsewhere in his work the point is as vigorously made in happier contexts. It will be remembered that the first of the Holmes short stories, which were to put him on the road to immortality, was a firm, almost brutal, assertion of his defeat at the hands of a woman.

The alcoholism of Charles Doyle and, it may be, a few wild nights with fellow-students on the part of Conan Doyle, give rise to another aspect of the stories: the terror of losing control of normal social impulses and destruction of self-respect. Only a minor character in "Cowles" is actually presented in a state of alcoholism,

4

but Cowles's own obsession is easily translated to — and from — that of a likeable person who cannot see his own doom in his love of alcohol. In the case of Gilroy, alcoholism and its effects form an even more obvious basis for what in the story is the Professor's irrationality under enchantment. Conan Doyle's writing reached a very sympathetic and involved audience during its frequent references to the proximity of struggling professionals to socio-economic destruction; his own family background had perpetually teetered on the verge of that brink; and Professor Gilroy's case turns on the terrible vulnerability of professional respectability, alcoholism being one of the most frequent threats to survival in that world. Experience of alcoholics and their treatment, even their attempts at self-treatment, certainly gave a grim quality to Gilroy's attempts to fight off the seductive power of his own enemy.

The other three items in this volume possess a different interest. The full M.D. dissertation which Conan Doyle wrote at Southsea and presented with success to Edinburgh University in 1885, is too large, too technical and, in part, too obsolete to justify inclusion in a popular work. But it merits brief quotation to exhibit a point hitherto ignored. If Doyle's medical knowledge lent a scientific basis and a tone of realism to his writing, whether in Holmes's consulting-room, medical-demonstration or surgeon-lecture techniques, or in the almost clinical presentation of certain characters, his own developing prowess as a writer of fiction made curious inroads on his medical research. One singular passage in his dissertation, presented here, shows a recital of symptoms gradually evolving into a biography of the patient, and a world of minor characters and background detail gradually coming alive in the doctoral candidate's mind. The scholar informed the writer; but the writer was struggling to break out of the scholar. A more predictable way in which the thesis would go on to influence future fictional work, particularly detective-work, is the later passage on a personal case-study based on an actual patient, and the charm of the irony with which Doyle concludes that portion of the narrative is both characteristic and highly suggestive. It also foreshadows those intriguing stories in which Conan Doyle presented his readers with a truncated conclusion, circumstances preventing the final clearing-up of the case — "A Case of Identity", "The Five Orange Pips", "The Engineer's Thumb", "The Resident Patient" and "The Greek Interpreter" being but a few, obvious, examples.

Among the many points in our extracts from the dissertation which throw new light on Conan Doyle's later writing is the coldly scientific citation of his research into remedial drugs by making experiments on himself to see how large a dose might safely be prescribed. It is a remarkable indication of the courage and dedication which he brought to his investigation and shows how deeply his scholarly enthusiasm and desire for the betterment of humanity dominated him. Here, certainly, is a clear revelation of Conan Doyle himself among the other human originals for Sherlock Holmes. Holmes's readiness to conduct experiments on himself was one of the first points made about him, and indeed is mentioned to Watson before he meets Holmes at all. But it is evident that Doyle's literary imagination as well as his retrospective reconsideration led him to reflect on the dangerous possible side-effects of experimentation with an overdose of drugs, and from this it was a short step to making Holmes a cocaine addict. A final use both of self-experimentation, and of subsequent remorse for the failure to consider other consequences of it in the fever of the chase, is made in the most horrific possible form in "The Devil's Foot", where Holmes and Watson nearly blast their own minds while attempting to discover the nature of the drug which killed Brenda and Mortimer Tregennis and drove into insanity their brothers George and Owen.

But it would be misleading to see Conan Doyle's writings for or about Edinburgh University and its staff and students as exclusively concerned with darker themes. His rich vein of comedy and irony found expression in far more of his work than has been generally recognised: much of the charm of the Holmes stories, for instance, derives from concealed as well as open humour, and the same is true of the bulk of his long and short stories. Of these latter a remarkable volume, *Round the Red Lamp*, published in 1894, was entirely concerned with medical life. It was natural that at least one of its stories should have been directly set in the atmosphere of his own student days. The date of its composition is uncertain: a few of its companion stories had been written some years previously, but most were previously unpublished and the confidence of style suggests that the theme recommended itself when he was writing the bulk of the stories for book publication. If, then, it comes from 1893-94, it is clear that his recollection of his world of some fifteen years earlier was excellent, and he evidently derived a nostalgic satisfaction in the mention of Rutherford's pub in Drummond Street, opposite Old

College. It is probable that some of the reactions of the younger student in the story were indeed Conan Doyle's own at first operation; but it seems likely that the actual incident, if it had a foundation in fact, befell a more nervous and suggestible student — of the relative weakness of will depicted in several protagonists elsewhere in this present collection. The little story is of considerable interest to the social historian, being clearly very close indeed to what normally transpired in Edinburgh operations before a student audience, and the casual conversation of the surgeon indicates a source for Holmes's small-talk to Watson in the intervals of discussing his cases — very notably during the chase led by the mongrel Toby in *The Sign of Four*.

And Sherlock Holmes himself was in fact brought directly into confrontation with Conan Doyle's Edinburgh in a story unknown to almost all readers of what they mistakenly took to be the complete Sherlock Holmes. The dissertation was not Conan Doyle's last offering to his old university. On November 20, 1896, the Edinburgh University *Student* appeared with a number of contributions from distinguished alumni and friends in furtherance of a charitable appeal (whose nature will present itself in the text). Sherlock Holmes had been formally buried in the Reichenbach in the *Strand* for December 1893, but in response to the call from the students, Conan Doyle resurrected him for a brief, frivolous moment: it would be five more years before *The Hound of the Baskervilles*, and two more yet before Holmes's divorce from Reichenbach was made absolute in *The Return of Sherlock Holmes*. Conan Doyle even wickedly headed his self-parody "The Field Bazaar" with the same title as the book publication of what he had intended to be the last Holmes stories: *The Memoirs of Sherlock Holmes*. It merits serious critical attention as a reminder of the intense amusement he derived from his own literary composition, part of the joke turning on self-identification with Watson in this little story (although there was much more of himself in Holmes than he troubled to assert). The apparent Englishness of Holmes (an Englishness less apparent to those who, like Doyle's family, heard his adventures read in the author's high Scottish intonation) led many interested commentators to puzzle *ad nauseam* as to whether Holmes had been to Oxford or Cambridge. In fact, Holmes's university career is clearly based on the university Doyle knew: but he only gives Edinburgh warrant for claiming Watson, albeit Holmes's awareness of university cash priorities suggests personal knowledge of the same institution. Anyhow, any university could congratulate itself on a pupil with the humanity, decency and literary genius of Watson.

It was eminently characteristic of Conan Doyle to respond with such generosity (and at some cost to his own wish for emancipation from Holmes) to the *Student's* appeal. Ten years ago *Student* became the basis for the creation of the Edinburgh University Student Publications Board, now directors of Polygon Books. It is, therefore, with the greatest pride and pleasure that we reprint the work given us by our most celebrated author. We express our thanks in the way he would most have wished, that of dedicating his gift to us, together with its accompanying Edinburgh works, to his surviving daughter, Dame Jean Conan Doyle, to whom, indeed, our own thanks are due for her very kind interest in the present book, and for several most helpful pieces of information which have been of great benefit to this introduction. We would also like to express our appreciation to Air Vice-Marshal Sir Geoffrey Bromet, to Professor W. W. Robson, to Mr Colin Affleck, to the National Library of Scotland, to the Edinburgh University Library (and especially its Keeper of Special Collections, Dr J. T. D. Hall), to Professor George Shepperson, to Mr Bill Campbell, and to the permanent staff of the Board, notably Mrs Magaret Roxton, Mr Neville Moir and Mr Adam Griffin. Mr Timothy Willis, Chairman of the Board, and research associate of the introducer, encouraged us throughout. Miss Louise Simson joined our operation most effectively at the proof-reading stage. Mr James Hutcheson took particular pains to give us a striking and imaginative cover-design.

Dr Graham Sutton, editor of the Board's medical journal, *Synapse*, very kindly undertook the work of reading the manuscript of the doctoral dissertation and of editing the material selected from it: the notes are his.

The publication of the book was directed by Mr Graham Richardson, despite his onerous duties as Honorary Treasurer of the Edinburgh University Students' Association. It has been a privilege to have worked under him in the enterprise, and I think Conan Doyle would be proud of him.

Department of History,
University of Edinburgh.   OWEN DUDLEY EDWARDS.

THE FIELD BAZAAR

"I SHOULD certainly do it," said Sherlock Holmes. I started at the interruption, for my companion had been eating his breakfast with his attention entirely centred upon the paper which was propped up by the coffee pot. Now I looked across at him to find his eyes fastened upon me with the half-amused, half-questioning expression which he usually assumed when he felt that he had made an intellectual point.

"Do what?" I asked.

He smiled as he took his slipper from the mantelpiece and drew from it enough shag tobacco to fill the old clay pipe with which he invariably rounded off his breakfast.

"A most characteristic question of yours, Watson," said he. "You will not, I am sure, be offended if I say that any reputation for sharpness which I may possess has been entirely gained by the admirable foil which you have made for me. Have I not heard of debutantes who have insisted upon plainness in their chaperones? There is a certain analogy."

Our long companionship in the Baker Street rooms had left us on those easy terms of intimacy when much may be said without offence. And yet I acknowledge that I was nettled at his remark.

"I may be very obtuse," said I, "but I confess that I am unable to see how you have managed to know that I was . . . I was . . ."

"Asked to help in the Edinburgh University Bazaar."

"Precisely. The letter has only just come to hand, and I have not spoken to you since."

"In spite of that," said Holmes, leaning back in his chair and putting his finger tips together. "I would even venture to suggest that the object of the bazaar is to enlarge the University cricket field."

I looked at him in such bewilderment that he vibrated with silent laughter.

"The fact is, my dear Watson, that you are an excellent subject," said he. "You are never *blasé*. You respond instantly to any external

9

stimulus. Your mental processes may be slow but they are never obscure, and I found during breakfast that you were easier reading than the leader in the *Times* in front of me."

"I should be glad to know how you arrived at your conclusions," said I.

"I fear that my good nature in giving explanations has seriously compromised my reputation," said Holmes. "But in this case the train of reasoning is based upon such obvious facts that no credit can be claimed for it. You entered the room with a thoughtful expression, the expression of a man who is debating some point in his mind. In your hand you held a solitary letter. Now last night you retired in the best of spirits, so it was clear that it was this letter in your hand which had caused the change in you."

"This is obvious."

"It is all obvious when it is explained to you. I naturally asked myself what the letter could contain which might have this effect upon you. As you walked you held the flap side of the envelope towards me, and I saw upon it the same shield-shaped device which I have observed upon your old college cricket cap. It was clear, then, that the request came from Edinburgh University — or from some club connected with the University. When you reached the table you laid down the letter beside your plate with the address uppermost, and you walked over to look at the framed photograph upon the left of the mantelpiece."

It amazed me to see the accuracy with which he had observed my movements. "What next?" I asked.

"I began by glancing at the address, and I could tell, even at the distance of six feet, that it was an official communication. This I gathered from the use of the word 'Doctor' upon the address, to which, as a Bachelor of Medicine, you have no legal claim. I knew that University officials are pedantic in their correct use of titles, and I was thus enabled to say with certainty that your letter was ·unofficial. When on your return to the table you turned over your letter and allowed me to perceive that the enclosure was a printed one, the idea of a bazaar first occurred to me. I had already weighed the possibility of its being a political communication, but this seemed improbable in the present stagnant condition of politics.

"When you returned to the table your face still retained its expression, and it was evident that your examination of the photograph had not changed the current of your thoughts. In that case it must itself bear upon the subject in question. I turned my attention to the photograph, therefore, and saw at once that it consisted of yourself as a member of the Edinburgh University Eleven, with the pavilion and cricket-field in the background. My small experience of cricket clubs has taught me that next to churches and cavalry ensigns they are the most debt-laden things upon earth. When upon your return to the table I saw you take out your pencil and draw lines upon the envelope, I was convinced that you were endeavouring to realise some projected improvement which was to be brought about by a bazaar. Your face still showed some indecision, so that I was able to break in upon you with my advice that you should assist in so good an object."

I could not help smiling at the extreme simplicity of his explanation.

"Of course, it was as easy as possible," said I.

My remark appeared to nettle him.

"I may add," said he, "that the particular help which you have been asked to give was that you should write in their album, and that you have already made up your mind that the present incident will be the subject of your article."

"But how ——!" I cried.

"It is as easy as possible," said he, "and I leave its solution to your own ingenuity. In the meantime," he added, raising his paper, "you will excuse me if I return to this very interesting article upon the trees of Cremona, and the exact reasons for their pre-eminence in the manufacture of violins. It is one of those small outlying problems to which I am sometimes tempted to direct my attention."

HIS FIRST OPERATION

IT was the first day of a winter session, and the third year's man was walking with the first year's man. Twelve o'clock just booming out from the Tron Church.

"Let me see," said the third year's man, "you have never seen an operation?"

"Never."

"Then this way, please. This is Rutherford's historic bar. A glass of sherry, please, for this gentleman. You are rather sensitive, are you not?"

"My nerves are not very strong, I am afraid."

"Hum! Another glass of sherry for this gentleman. We are going to an operation now, you know."

The novice squared his shoulders and made a gallant attempt to look unconcerned.

"Nothing very bad — eh?"

"Well, yes — pretty bad."

"An — an amputation?"

"No, it's a bigger affair than that."

"I think — I think they must be expecting me at home."

"There's no sense funking. If you don't go today you must tomorrow. Better get it over at once. Feel pretty fit?"

"Oh, yes, all right."

The smile was not a success.

"One more glass of sherry, then. Now come on or we shall be late. I want you to be well in front."

"Surely that is not necessary."

"Oh, it is far better. What a drove of students! There are plenty of new men among them. You can tell them easily enough, can't you? If they were going down to be operated upon themselves they could not look whiter."

"I don't think I should look as white."

"Well, I was just the same myself. But the feeling soon wears off. You see a fellow with a face like plaster, and before the week is out

13

he is eating his lunch in the dissecting rooms. I'll tell you all about the case when we get to the theatre."

The students were pouring down the sloping street which led to the infirmary — each with his little sheaf of notebooks in his hand. There were pale, frightened lads, fresh from the High Schools, and callous old chronics, whose generation had passed on and left them. They swept in an unbroken, tumultuous stream from the University gate to the hospital. The figures and gait of the men were young, but there was little youth in most of their faces. Some looked as if they ate too little — a few as if they drank too much. Tall and short, tweed coated and black, round-shouldered, bespectacled and slim, they crowded with clatter of feet and rattle of sticks through the hospital gate. Now and again they thickened into two lines as the carriage of a surgeon of the staff rolled over the cobblestones between.

"There's going to be a crowd at Archer's," whispered the senior man with suppressed excitement. "It is grand to see him at work. I've seen him jab all round the aorta until it made me jumpy to watch him. This way, and mind the whitewash."

They passed under an archway and down a long, stone-flagged corridor with drab-coloured doors on either side, each marked with a number. Some of them were ajar, and the novice glanced into them with tingling nerves. He was reassured to catch a glimpse of cheery fires, lines of white-counterpaned beds and a profusion of coloured texts upon the wall. The corridor opened upon a small hall with a fringe of poorly-clad people seated all round upon benches. A young man with a pair of scissors stuck, like a flower, in his button-hole, and a notebook in his hand, was passing from one to the other, whispering and writing.

"Anything good?" asked the third year's man.

"You should have been here yesterday," said the out-patient clerk, glancing up. "We had a regular field day. A popliteal aneurism, a Colles' fracture, a spina bifida, a tropical abscess, and an elephantiasis. How's that for a single haul?"

"I'm sorry I missed it. But they'll come again, I suppose. What's up with the old gentleman?"

A broken workman was sitting in the shadow, rocking himself slowly to and fro and groaning. A woman beside him was trying to console him, patting his shoulder with a hand which was spotted over with curious little white blisters.

"It's a fine carbuncle," said the clerk, with the air of a connoisseur

14

who describes his orchids to one who can appreciate them. "It's on his back, and the passage is draughty, so we must not look at it, must we, daddy? Pemphigus," he added carelessly, pointing to the woman's disfigured hands. "Would you care to stop and take out a metacarpal?"

"No thank you, we are due at Archer's. Come on;" and they rejoined the throng which was hurrying to the theatre of the famous surgeon.

The tiers of horseshoe benches, rising from the floor to the ceiling, were already packed, and the novice as he entered saw vague, curving lines of faces in front of him, and heard the deep buzz of a hundred voices and sounds of laughter from somewhere up above him. His companion spied an opening on the second bench, and they both sqeezed into it.

"This is grand," the senior man whispered; "you'll have a rare view of it all."

Only a single row of heads intervened between them and the operating table. It was of unpainted deal, plain, strong and scrupulously clean. A sheet of brown waterproofing covered half of it, and beneath stood a large tin tray full of sawdust. On the further side, in front of the window, there was a board which was strewed with glittering instruments, forceps, tenacula, saws, canulas and trocars. A line of knives, with long, thin, delicate blades, lay at one side. Two young men lounged in front of this; one threading needles, the other doing something to a brass coffee-pot-like thing which hissed out puffs of steam.

"That's Peterson," whispered the senior. "The big, bald man in the front row. He's the skin-grafting man, you know. And that's Anthony Browne, who took a larynx out successfully last winter. And there's Murphy the pathologist, and Stoddart the eye man. You'll come to know them all soon."

"Who are the two men at the table?"

"Nobody — dressers. One has charge of the instruments and the other of the puffing Billy. It's Lister's antiseptic spray, you know, and Archer's one of the carbolic acid men. Hayes is the leader of the cleanliness-and-cold-water school, and they all hate each other like poison."

A flutter of interest passed through the closely-packed benches as a woman in petticoat and bodice was led in by two nurses. A red woollen shawl was draped over her head and round her neck. The

15

face which looked out from it was that of a woman in the prime of her years, but drawn with suffering and of a peculiar bees-wax tint. Her head drooped as she walked, and one of the nurses, with her arm round her waist, was whispering consolation in her ear. She gave a quick side glance at the instrument table as she passed, but the nurses turned her away from it.

"What ails her?" asked the novice.

"Cancer of the parotid. It's the devil of a case, extends right away back behind the carotids. There's hardly a man but Archer would dare to follow it. Ah, here he is himself."

As he spoke, a small, brisk, iron-grey man came striding into the room, rubbing his hands together as he walked. He had a clean-shaven face of the naval officer type, with large, bright eyes, and a firm, straight mouth. Behind him came his big house surgeon with his gleaming pince-nez and a trail of dressers, who grouped themselves into the corners of the room.

"Gentlemen," cried the surgeon in a voice as hard and brisk as his manner. "We have here an interesting case of tumour of the parotid, originally cartilaginous but now assuming malignant characteristics, and therefore requiring excision. On to the table, nurse! Thank you! Chloroform, clerk! Thank you! You can take the shawl off, nurse."

The woman lay back upon the waterproofed pillow and her murderous tumour lay revealed. In itself it was a pretty thing, ivory white with a mesh of blue veins, and curving gently from jaw to chest. But the lean, yellow face, and the stringy throat were in horrible contrast with the plumpness and sleekness of this monstrous growth. The surgeon placed a hand on each side of it and pressed it slowly backwards and forwards.

"Adherent at one place, gentlemen," he cried. "The growth involves the carotids and jugulars, and passes behind the ramus of the jaw, whither we must be prepared to follow it. It is impossible to say how deep our dissection may carry us. Carbolic tray, thank you! Dressings of carbolic gauze, if you please! Push the chloroform, Mr Johnson. Have the small saw ready in case it is necessary to remove the jaw."

The patient was moaning gently under the towel which had been placed over her face. She tried to raise her arms and to draw up her knees but two dressers restrained her. The heavy air was full of the penetrating smells of carbolic acid and of chloroform. A muffled cry came from under the towel and then a snatch of a song, sung in a high, quavering, monotonous voice.

> He says, says he,
> If you fly with me
>> You'll be mistress of the ice-cream van;
>> You'll be mistress of the–

It mumbled off into a drone and stopped. The surgeon came across, still rubbing his hands, and spoke to an elderly man in front of the novice.

"Narrow squeak for the Government," he said.

"Oh, ten is enough."

"They won't have ten long. They'd do better to resign before they are driven to it."

"Oh, I should fight it out."

"What's the use. They can't get past the committee, even if they get a vote in the House. I was talking to—"

"Patient's ready, sir," said the dresser.

"Talking to M'Donald — but I'll tell you about it presently." He walked back to the patient, who was breathing in long, heavy gasps. "I propose," said he, passing his hand over the tumour in an almost caressing fashion, "to make a free incision over the posterior border and to take another forward at right angles to the lower end of it. Might I trouble you for a medium knife, Mr Johnson."

The novice, with eyes which were dilating with horror, saw the surgeon pick up the long, gleaming knife, dip it into a tin basin and balance it in his fingers as an artist might his brush. Then he saw him pinch up the skin above the tumour with his left hand. At the sight, his nerves, which had already been tried once or twice that day, gave way utterly. His head swam round and he felt that in another instant he might faint. He dared not look at the patient. He dug his thumbs into his ears lest some scream should come to haunt him, and he fixed his eyes rigidly upon the wooden ledge in front of him. One glance, one cry, would, he knew, break down the shred of self-possession which he still retained. He tried to think of cricket, of green fields and rippling water, of his sisters at home — of anything rather than of what was going on so near him.

And yet, somehow, even with his ears stopped up, sounds seemed to penetrate to him and to carry their own tale. He heard, or thought that he heard, the long hissing of the carbolic engine. Then he was conscious of some movement among the dressers. Were there groans

17

too breaking in upon him, and some other sound, some fluid sound which was more dreadfully suggestive still? His mind would keep building up every step of the operation, and fancy made it more ghastly than fact could have been. His nerves tingled and quivered. Minute by minute the giddiness grew more marked, the numb, sickly feeling at his heart more distressing. And then suddenly, with a groan, his head pitching forward and his brow cracking sharply upon the narrow, wooden shelf in front of him, he lay in a dead faint.

When he came to himself he was lying in the empty theatre with his collar and shirt undone. The third year's man was dabbing a wet sponge over his face, and a couple of grinning dressers were looking on.

"All right," cried the novice, sitting up and rubbing his eyes; "I'm sorry to have made an ass of myself."

"Well, so I should think," said his companion. "What on earth did you faint about?"

"I couldn't help it. It was that operation."

"What operation?"

"Why, that cancer "

There was a pause, and then the three students burst out laughing.

"Why, you juggins," cried the senior man, "there never was an operation at all. They found the patient didn't stand the chloroform well, and so the whole thing was off. Archer has been giving us one of his racy lectures, and you fainted just in the middle of his favourite story."

JOHN BARRINGTON COWLES

PART I

IT might seem rash of me to say that I ascribe the death of my poor friend, John Barrington Cowles, to any preternatural agency. I am aware that in the present state of public feeling a chain of evidence would require to be strong indeed before the possibility of such a conclusion could be admitted.

I shall therefore merely state the circumstances which led up to this sad event as concisely and as plainly as I can, and leave every reader to draw his own deductions. Perhaps there may be someone who can throw light upon what is dark to me.

I first met Barrington Cowles when I went up to Edinburgh University to take out medical classes there. My landlady in Northumberland Street had a large house, and being a widow without children, she gained a livelihood by providing accommodations for several students.

Barrington Cowles happened to have taken a bedroom upon the same floor as mine, and when we came to know each other better we shared a small sitting-room, in which we took our meals. In this manner we originated a friendship which was unmarred by the slightest disagreement up to the day of his death.

Cowles' father was the colonel of a Sikh regiment and had remained in India for many years. He allowed his son a handsome income, but seldom gave any other sign of parental affection — writing irregularly and briefly.

My friend, who had himself been born in India, and whose whole disposition was an ardent, tropical one, was much hurt by this neglect. His mother was dead, and he had no other relation in the world to supply the blank.

Thus he came in time to concentrate all his affection upon me, and to confide in me in a manner which is rare among men. Even when a

19

stronger and deeper passion came upon him, it never infringed upon the old tenderness between us.

Cowles was a tall, slim young fellow, with an olive, Velasquez-like face, and dark, tender eyes. I have seldom seen a man who was more likely to excite a woman's interest or to captivate her imagination. His expression was, as a rule, dreamy, and even languid; but if in conversation a subject arose which interested him, he would be all animation in a moment. On such occasions his colour would heighten, his eyes gleam, and he could speak with an eloquence which would carry his audience with him.

In spite of these natural advantages he led a solitary life, avoiding female society, and reading with great diligence. He was one of the foremost men of his year, taking the senior medal for anatomy, and the Neil Arnott prize for physics.

How well I can recollect the first time we met her! Often and often I have recalled the circumstances, and tried to remember what the exact impression was which she produced on my mind at the time. After we came to know her, my judgment was warped, so that I am curious to recollect what my unbiased instincts were. It is hard, however, to eliminate the feelings which reason or prejudice afterward raised in me.

It was at the opening of the Royal Scottish Academy in the spring of 1879. My poor friend was passionately attached to art in every form, and a pleasing chord in music or a delicate effect upon canvas would give exquisite pleasure to his highly strung nature. We had gone together to see the pictures, and were standing in the grand central *salon* when I noticed an extremely beautiful woman standing at the other side of the room. In my whole life I have never seen such a classically perfect countenance. It was the real Greek type — the forehead broad, very low, and as white as marble, with a cloudlet of delicate locks wreathing round it, the nose straight and clean-cut, the lips inclined to thinness, the chin and lower jaw beautifully rounded off, and yet sufficiently developed to promise unusual strength of character.

But those eyes — those wonderful eyes! If I could but give some faint idea of their varying moods, their steely hardness, their feminine softness, their power of command, their penetrating intensity suddenly melting away into an expression of womanly weakness — but I am speaking now of future impressions!

There was a tall, yellow-haired young man with this lady, whom I at once recognised as a law student with whom I had a slight acquaintance.

Archibald Reeves — for that was his name — was a dashing, handsome young fellow, and had at one time been a ringleader in every university escapade; but of late I had seen little of him, and the report was that he was engaged to be married. His companion was, then, I presumed, his *fiancée*. I seated myself upon the velvet settee in the centre of the room and furtively watched the couple from behind my catalogue.

The more I looked at her the more her beauty grew upon me. She was somewhat short in stature, it is true; but her figure was perfection, and she bore herself in such a fashion that it was only by actual comparison that one would have known her to be under the medium height.

As I kept my eyes upon them, Reeves was called away for some reason, and the young lady was left alone. Turning her back to the picture, she passed the time until the return of her escort in taking a deliberate survey of the company, without paying the least heed to the fact that a dozen pairs of eyes, attracted by her elegance and beauty, were bent curiously upon her. With one of her hands holding the red silk cord which railed off the pictures, she stood languidly moving her eyes from face to face with as little self-consciousness as if she were looking at the canvas creatures behind her. Suddenly, as I watched her, I saw her gaze become fixed, and, as it were, intense. I followed the direction of her looks, wondering what could have attracted her so strongly.

John Barrington Cowles was standing before a picture — one, I think, by Noel Paton — I know that the subject was a noble and ethereal one. His profile was turned towards us, and never have I seen him to such advantage. I have said that he was a strikingly handsome man, but at that moment he looked absolutely magnificent. It was evident that he had momentarily forgotten his surroundings, and that his whole soul was in sympathy with the picture before him. His eyes sparkled, and a dusky pink shone through his clear, olive cheeks. She continued to watch him fixedly, with a look of interest upon her face, until he came out of his reverie with a start, and turned abruptly round, so that his gaze met hers. She glanced away at once, but his eyes remained fixed upon her for some moments. The picture was forgotten already, and his soul had come down to earth once more.

We caught sight of her once or twice before we left, and each time I noticed my friend look after her. He made no remark, however, until we got out into the open air, and were walking arm in arm along Princes Street.

"Did you notice that beautiful woman, in the dark dress, with the white fur?" he asked.

"Yes, I saw her," I answered.

"Do you know her?" he asked, eagerly. "Have you any idea who she is?"

"I don't know her personally," I replied. "But I have no doubt I could find out all about her, for I believe she is engaged to young Archie Reeves, and he and I have a lot of mutual friends."

"Engaged!" ejaculated Cowles.

"Why, my dear boy," I said, laughing, "you don't mean to say you are so susceptible that the fact that a girl to whom you never spoke in your life is engaged is enough to upset you?"

"Well, not exactly to upset me," he answered, forcing a laugh. "But I don't mind telling you, Armitage, that I never was so taken by anyone in my life. It wasn't the mere beauty of the face — though that was perfect enough — but it was the character and the intellect upon it. I hope, if she is engaged, that it is to some man who will be worthy of her."

"Why," I remarked, "you speak quite feelingly. It is a clear case of love at first sight, Jack. However, to put your perturbed spirit at rest, I'll make a point of finding out all about her whenever I meet any fellow who is likely to know."

Barrington Cowles thanked me, and the conversation drifted off into other channels. For several days neither of us made any allusion to the subject, though my companion was perhaps a little more dreamy and distraught than usual. The incident had almost vanished from my remembrance, when one day young Brodie, who is a second cousin of mine, came up to me on the university steps with the face of a bearer of tidings.

"I say," he began, "you know Reeves, don't you?"

"Yes. What of him?"

"His engagement is off."

"Off!" I cried. "Why, I only learned the other day that it was on."

"Oh, yes — it's all off. His brother told me so. Deucedly mean of Reeves, you know, if he has backed out of it, for she was an uncommonly nice girl."

"I've seen her," I said; "but I don't know her name."

"She is a Miss Northcott, and lives with an old aunt of hers in Abercrombie Place. Nobody knows anything about her people, or where she comes from. Anyhow, she is about the most unlucky girl in the world, poor soul!"

"Why unlucky?"

"Well, you know, this was her second engagement," said young Brodie, who had a marvellous knack of knowing everything about everybody. "She was engaged to Prescott — William Prescott, who died. That was a very sad affair. The wedding-day was fixed, and the whole thing looked as straight as a die when the smash came."

"What smash?" I asked, with some dim recollection of the circumstances.

"Why, Prescott's death. He came to Abercrombie Place one night, and stayed very late. No one knows exactly when he left, but about one in the morning a fellow who knew him met him walking rapidly in the direction of the Queen's Park. He bid him goodnight, but Prescott hurried on without heeding him, and that was the last time he was ever seen alive. Three days afterward his body was found floating in St. Margaret's Loch, under St. Anthony's Chapel. No one could ever understand it, but of course the verdict brought it in as temporary insanity."

"It was very strange," I remarked.

"Yes, and deucedly rough on the poor girl," said Brodie. "Now that this other blow has come it will quite crush her. So gentle and ladylike she is, too!"

"You know her personally, then?" I asked.

"Oh, yes, I know her. I have met her several times. I could easily manage that you should be introduced to her."

"Well," I answered, "it's not so much for my own sake as for a friend of mine. However, I don't suppose she will go out much for some little time after this. When she does, I will take advantage of your offer."

We shook hands on this, and I thought no more of the matter for some time.

The next incident which I have to relate as bearing at all upon the question of Miss Northcott is an unpleasant one. Yet I must detail it as accurately as possible, since it may throw some light upon the sequel. One cold night, several months after the conversation with my second cousin which I have quoted above, I was walking down one of the lowest streets in the city on my way back from a case which I had been attending. It was very late, and I was picking my way among the dirty loungers who were clustering round the doors of a great gin-palace, when a man staggered out from among them, and held out his hand to me with a drunken leer. The gaslight fell full upon his face, and, to my intense astonishment, I recognised in the degraded creature before me my former acquaintance, young Archibald Reeves, who had once been famous as one of the most dressy and particular men in the whole college. I was so utterly surprised that for a moment I almost doubted the evidence of my own senses; but there was no mistaking those features, which, though bloated with drink, still retained something of their former comeliness. I was determined to rescue him, for one night at least, from the company into which he had fallen.

"Halloo, Reeves!" I said. "Come along with me. I'm going in your direction."

He muttered some incoherent apology for his condition, and took my arm. As I supported him toward his lodgings, I could see that he was not only suffering from the effects of a recent debauch, but that a long course of intemperance had affected his nerves and his brain. His hand when I touched it was dry and feverish, and he started from every shadow which fell upon the pavement. He rambled in his speech, too, in a manner which suggested the delirium of disease rather than the talk of a drunkard.

When I got him to his lodgings, I partially undressed him and laid him upon his bed. His pulse at this time was very high, and he was evidently extremely feverish. He seemed to have sunk into a doze; and I was about to steal out of the room to warn his landlady of his condition, when he started up and caught me by the sleeve of my coat.

"Don't go!" he cried. "I feel better when you are here. I am safe from her then."

"From her!" I said. "From whom?"

"Her! her!" he answered peevishly. "Ah! you don't know her. She is the devil! Beautiful — beautiful; but the devil!"

"You are feverish and excited," I said. "Try and get a little sleep. You will wake better."

"Sleep!" he groaned. "How am I to sleep when I see her sitting down yonder at the foot of the bed with her great eyes watching and watching hour after hour? I tell you it saps all the strength and manhood out of me. That's what makes me drink. God help me — I'm half drunk now!"

"You are very ill," I said, putting some vinegar to his temples; "and you are delirious. You don't know what you say."

"Yes, I do," he interrupted, sharply, looking up at me. "I know very well what I say. I brought it upon myself. It is my own choice. But I couldn't — no, by Heaven! I couldn't — accept the alternative. I couldn't keep my faith with her. It was more than man could do."

I sat by the side of the bed, holding one of his burning hands in mine, and wondering over his strange words. He lay still for some time, and then, raising his eyes to me, said in a most plaintive voice:

"Why did she not give me warning sooner? Why did she wait until I had learned to love her so?"

He repeated this question several times, rolling his feverish head from side to side, and then he dropped into a troubled sleep. I crept out of the room, and, having seen that he would be properly cared for, left the house. His words, however, rang in my ears for days afterward, and assumed a deeper significance when taken with what was to come.

My friend, Barrington Cowles, had been away for his summer holidays, and I had heard nothing of him for several months. When the winter session came on, however, I received a telegram from him, asking me to secure the old rooms in Northumberland Street for him, and telling me the train by which he would arrive. I went down to meet him, and was delighted to find him looking wonderfully hearty and well.

"By the way," he said, suddenly, that night, as we sat in our chairs by the fire, talking over the events of the holidays, "you have never congratulated me yet!"

"On what, my boy?" I asked.

"What! Do you mean to say you have not heard of my engagement?"

"Engagement! No!" I answered. "However, I am delighted to hear it, and congratulate you with all my heart."

"I wonder it didn't come to your ears," he said. "It was the queerest thing. You remember that girl whom we both admired so much at the Academy?"

"What!" I cried, with a vague feeling of apprehension at my heart. "You don't mean to say that you are engaged to her?"

"I thought you would be surprised," he answered. "When I was staying with an old aunt of mine in Peterhead, in Aberdeenshire, the Northcotts happened to come there on a visit, and as we had mutual friends we soon met. I found out that it was a false alarm about her being engaged, and then — well, you know what it is when you are thrown into the society of such a girl in a place like Peterhead. Not, mind you," he added, "that I consider I did a foolish or hasty thing. I have never regretted it for a moment. The more I know Kate the more I admire her and love her. However, you must be introduced to her, and then you will form your own opinion."

I expressed my pleasure at the prospect, and endeavoured to speak as lightly as I could to Cowles upon the subject, but I felt depressed and anxious at heart. The words of Reeves and the unhappy fate of young Prescott recurred to my recollection, and though I could assign no tangible reason for it, a vague, dim fear and distrust of the woman took possession of me. It may be that this was a foolish prejudice and superstition upon my part, and that I involuntarily contorted her future doings and sayings to fit into some half-formed wild theory of my own. This has been suggested to me by others as an explanation of my narrative. They are welcome to their opinion if they can reconcile it with the facts which I have to tell.

I went round with my friend a few days afterward to call upon Miss Northcott. I remember that, as we went down Abercrombie Place, our attention was attracted by the shrill yelping of a dog, which noise proved eventually to come from the house to which we were bound. We were shown upstairs, where I was introduced to old Mrs Merton, Miss Northcott's aunt, and to the young lady herself. She looked as beautiful as ever, and I could not wonder at my friend's infatuation. Her face was a little more flushed than usual, and she held in her hand a heavy dog-whip, with which she had been chastising a small Scotch terrier, whose cries we had heard in the street. The poor brute was cringing up against the wall, whining piteously, and evidently completely cowed.

"So, Kate," said my friend, after we had taken our seats, "you have been falling out with Carlo again."

"Only a very little quarrel this time," she said, smiling charmingly. "He is a dear, good old fellow, but he needs correction now and then." Then, turning to me, "We all do that, Mr Armitage, don't we? What a capital thing if, instead of receiving a collective punishment at the end our lives, we were to have one at once, as the dogs do, when we did anything wicked. It would make us more careful, wouldn't it?"

I acknowledged that it would.

"Supposing that every time a man misbehaved himself a gigantic hand were to seize him, and he were lashed with a whip until he fainted" — she clenched her white fingers as she spoke, and cut viciously with the dog-whip — " it would do more to keep him good than any number of high-minded theories of morality."

"Why, Kate," said my friend, "you are quite savage today."

"No, Jack," she laughed. "I'm only propounding a theory for Mr Armitage's consideration."

The two began to chat together about some Aberdeenshire reminiscence, and I had time to observe Mrs Merton, who had remained silent during our short conversation. She was a very strange-looking old lady. What attracted attention most in her appearance was the utter want of colour which she exhibited. Her hair was snow-white, and her face extremely pale. Her lips were bloodless, and even her eyes were such a light tinge of blue that they hardly relieved the general pallor. Her dress was a gray silk, which harmonised with her general appearance. She had a peculiar expression of countenance, which I was unable at the moment to refer to its proper cause. She was working at some old-fashioned piece of ornamental needlework, and as she moved her arms her dress gave forth a dry, melancholy rustling, like the sound of leaves in the autumn. There was something mournful and depressing in the sight of her. I moved my chair a little nearer, and asked her how she liked Edinburgh, and whether she had been there long.

When I spoke to her she started and looked up at me with a scared look on her face. Then I saw in a moment what the expression was which I had observed there. It was one of fear — intense and overpowering fear. It was so marked that I could have staked my life on the woman before me having at some period of her life been subjected to some terrible experience or dreadful misfortune.

"Oh, yes, I like it," she said, in a soft, timid voice; "and we have been here long — that is, not very long. We move about a great deal." She spoke with hesitation, as if afraid of committing herself.

"You are a native of Scotland, I presume?" I said.

"No — that is, not entirely. We are not natives of any place. We are cosmopolitan, you know." She glanced round in the direction of Miss Northcott as she spoke, but the two were still chatting together near the window. Then she suddenly bent forward to me, with a look of intense earnestness upon her face, and said:

"Don't talk to me anymore, please. She does not like it, and I shall suffer for it afterward. Please don't do it."

I was about to ask her the reason for this strange request, but when she saw I was going to address her, she rose and walked slowly out of the room. As she did so, I perceived that the lovers had ceased to talk, and that Miss Northcott was looking at me with her keen, gray eyes.

"You must excuse my aunt, Mr Armitage," she said; "she is old, and easily fatigued. Come over and look at my album."

We spent some time examining the portraits. Miss Northcott's father and mother were apparently ordinary mortals enough, and I could not detect in either of them any traces of the character which showed itself in their daughter's face. There was one old daguerreotype, however, which arrested my attention. It represented a man of about the age of forty, and strikingly handsome. He was clean shaven, and extraordinary power was expressed upon his prominent lower jaw and firm, straight mouth. His eyes were somewhat deeply set in his head, however, and there was a snake-like flattening at the upper part of his forehead, which detracted from his appearance. I almost involuntarily, when I saw the head, pointed to it, and exclaimed:

"There is your prototype in your family, Miss Northcott."

"Do you think so?" she said. "I am afraid you are paying me a very bad compliment. Uncle Anthony was always considered the black sheep of the family."

"Indeed," I answered; "my remark was an unfortunate one, then."

"Oh, don't mind that," she said; "I always thought myself that he was worth all of them put together. He was an officer in the Forty-first Regiment, and he was killed in action during the Persian War — so he died nobly, at any rate."

"That's the sort of death I should like to die," said Cowles, his dark eyes flashing, as they would when he was excited; "I often wish I had taken to my father's profession instead of this vile pill-compounding drudgery."

"Come, Jack, you are not going to die any sort of death yet," she said, tenderly taking his hand in hers.

I could not understand the woman. There was such an extraordinary mixture of masculine decision and womanly tenderness about her, with the consciousness of something all her own in the background, that she fairly puzzled me. I hardly knew, therefore, how to answer Cowles when, as we walked down the street together, he asked the comprehensive question:

"Well, what do you think of her?"

"I think she is wonderfully beautiful," I answered, guardedly.

"That, of course," he replied, irritably. "You knew that before you came!"

"I think she is very clever, too," I remarked.

Barrington Cowles walked on for some time, and then he suddenly turned on me with the strange question:

"Do you think she is cruel? Do you think she is the sort of girl who would take pleasure in inflicting pain?"

"Well, really," I answered, "I have hardly had time to form an opinion."

We then walked on for some time in silence.

"She is an old fool," at length muttered Cowles. "She is mad."

"Who is?" I asked.

"Why, that old woman — that aunt of Kate's — Mrs Merton, or whatever her name is."

Then I knew that my poor, colourless friend had been speaking to Cowles, but he never said anything more as to the nature of her communication.

My companion went to bed early that night, and I sat up a long time by the fire, thinking over all that I had seen and heard. I felt that there was some mystery about the girl — some dark fatality so strange as to defy conjecture. I thought of Prescott's interview with her before their marriage, and the fatal termination of it. I coupled it with poor, drunken Reeves' plaintive cry, "Why did she not tell me sooner?" and with the other words he had spoken. Then my mind ran over Mrs Merton's warning to me, and Cowles' reference to her, and even the episode of the whip and the cringing dog.

The whole effect of my recollections was unpleasant to a degree, and yet there was no tangible charge which I could bring against the woman. It would be worse than useless to attempt to warn my friend until I had definitely made up my mind what I was to warn him against. He would treat any charge against her with scorn. What could I do? How could I get at some tangible conclusion as to her character and antecedents? No one in Edinburgh knew them except as recent acquaintances. She was an orphan, and, as far as I knew, she had never disclosed where her former home had been. Suddenly an idea struck me. Among my father's friends there was a Colonel Joyce, who had served a long time in India upon the staff, and who would be likely to know most of the officers who had been out there since the Mutiny. I sat down at once, and, having trimmed the lamp, proceeded to write a letter to the colonel. I told him that I was very curious to gain some particulars about a certain Captain Northcott, who had served in the Forty-first Foot, and who had fallen in the Persian War. I described the man as well as I could from my recollection of the daguerreotype, and then, having directed the letter, posted it that very night, after which, feeling that I had done all that could be done, I retired to bed, with a mind too anxious to allow me to sleep.

PART II

I GOT an answer from Leicester, where the colonel resided, within two days. I have it before me as I write, and copy it verbatim.

"DEAR BOB," it said, "I remember the man well. I was with him at Calcutta, and afterward at Hyderabad. He was a curious, solitary sort of mortal; but a gallant soldier enough, for he distinguished himself at Sobraon, and was wounded, if I remember right. He was not popular in his corps — they said he was a pitiless, cold-blooded fellow, with no geniality in him. There was a rumour, too, that he was a devil-worshipper, or something of that sort, and also that he had the evil eye, which, of course, was all nonsense. He had some strange theories, I remember, about the power of the human will and the effect of mind upon matter.

"How are you getting on with your medical studies? Never forget, my boy, that your father's son has every claim upon me, and that if I can serve you in any way I am always at your command.

"Ever affectionately yours,

"EDWARD JOYCE.

"P.S.—By the way, Northcott did not fall in action. He was killed after peace was declared in a crazy attempt to get some of the eternal fire from the sun-worshippers' temple. There was considerable mystery about his death."

I read this epistle over several times — at first with a feeling of satisfaction, and then with one of disappointment. I had come on some curious information, and yet hardly what I wanted. He was an eccentric man, a devil-worshipper, and rumoured to have the power of the evil eye. I could believe the young lady's eyes, when endowed with that cold, gray shimmer which I had noticed in them once or twice, to be capable of any evil which human eye ever wrought; but still the superstition was an effete one. Was there not more meaning in that sentence which followed — "He had theories of the power of the human will and of the effect of mind upon matter"? I remember having once read a quaint treatise, which I had imagined to be mere charlatanism at the time, of the power of certain human minds, and of effects produced by them at a distance. Was Miss Northcott endowed with some exceptional power of the sort? The idea grew upon me, and very shortly I had evidence which convinced me of the truth of the supposition.

It happened that at the very time when my mind was dwelling upon this subject, I saw a notice in the paper that our town was to be visited by Doctor Messinger, the well-known medium and mesmerist. Messinger was a man whose performance, such as it was, had been again and again pronounced to be genuine by competent judges. He was far above trickery, and had the reputation of being the soundest living authority upon the strange pseudo-sciences of animal magnetism and electro-biology. Determined, therefore, to see what the human will could do, even against all the disadvantages of glaring footlights and a public platform, I took a ticket for the first night of the performance, and went with several student friends.

We had secured one of the side boxes, and did not arrive until after the performance had begun. I had hardly taken my seat before I recognised Barrington Cowles, with his *fiancée* and old Mrs Merton, sitting in the third or fourth row of the stalls. They caught sight of me at almost the same moment, and we bowed to each other. The first portion of the lecture was somewhat commonplace, the lecturer giving tricks of pure legerdemain, with one or two manifestations of mesmerism, performed upon a subject whom he had brought with him. He gave us an exhibition of clairvoyance, too, throwing his subject into a trance, and then demanding particulars as to the movements of absent friends, and the whereabouts of hidden objects, all of which appeared to be answered satisfactorily. I had seen all this before, however. What I wanted to see now was the effect of the lecturer's will when exerted upon some independent member of the audience.

He came round to that as the concluding exhibition in his performance. "I have shown you," he said, "that a mesmerised subject is entirely dominated by the will of the mesmeriser. He loses all power of volition, and his very thoughts are such as are suggested to him by the master mind. The same end may be attained without any preliminary process. A strong will can, simply by virtue of its strength, take possession of a weaker one, even at a distance, and can regulate the impulses and the actions of the owner of it. If there was one man in the world who had a very much more highly developed will than any of the rest of the human family, there is no reason why he should not be able to rule over them all, and to reduce his fellow-creatures to the condition of automatons. Happily there is such a dead level of mental power, or, rather, of mental weakness, among us that such a catastrophe is not likely to occur; but still within our small compass there are variations which produce surprising effects. I shall now single out one of the audience, and endeavour 'by the mere power of will' to compel him to come upon the platform, and do and say what I wish. Let me assure you that there is no collusion, and that the subject whom I may select is at perfect liberty to resent to the uttermost any impulse which I may communicate to him."

With these words the lecturer came to the front of the platform, and glanced over the first few rows of the stalls. No doubt Cowles' dark skin and bright eyes marked him out as a man of a highly nervous temperament, for the mesmerist picked him out in a moment, and fixed his eyes upon him. I saw my friend give a start of surprise, and then settle down in his chair, as if to express his determination not to yield to the influence of the operator. Messinger was not a man whose head denoted any great brainpower, but his gaze was singularly intense and penetrating. Under the influence of it Cowles made one or two spasmodic motions of his hands, as if to grasp the sides of his seat, and then half rose, but only to sink down again, though with an evident effort. I was watching the scene with intense interest, when I happened to catch a glimpse of Miss Northcott's face. She was sitting with her eyes fixed intently upon the mesmerist, and with such an expression of concentrated power upon her features as I have never seen on any other human countenance. Her jaw was firmly set, her lips compressed, and her face as hard as if it were a beautiful sculpture cut out of the whitest marble. Her eyebrows were drawn down, however, and from beneath them her gray eyes seemed to sparkle and gleam with a cold light.

I looked at Cowles again, expecting every moment to see him rise and obey the mesmerist's wishes, when there came from the platform a short, gasping cry of a man utterly worn out and prostrated by a prolonged struggle. Messinger was leaning against the table, his hand to his forehead, and the perspiration pouring down his face. "I won't go on," he cried, addressing the audience. "There is a stronger will than mine acting against me. You must excuse me for tonight." The man was evidently ill, and utterly unable to proceed, so the curtain was lowered, and the audience dispersed, with many comments on the lecturer's sudden indisposition.

I waited outside the hall until my friend and the ladies came out. Cowles was laughing over his recent experience.

"He didn't succeed with me, Bob," he cried, triumphantly, as he shook my hand. "I think he caught a Tartar that time."

"Yes," said Miss Northcott, "I think Jack ought to be very proud of his strength of mind; don't you, Mr Armitage?"

"It took me all my time, though," my friend said, seriously. "You can't conceive what a strange feeling I had once or twice. All the strength seemed to have gone out of me — especially just before he collapsed himself."

I walked round with Cowles in order to see the ladies home. He walked in front with Mrs Merton, and I found myself behind with the young lady. For a minute or so I walked beside her without making any remark, and then I suddenly blurted out, in a manner which must have seemed somewhat brusque to her:

"You did that, Miss Northcott."

"Did what?" she asked, sharply.

"Why, mesmerised the mesmeriser — I suppose that is the best way of describing the transaction."

"What a strange idea!" she said, laughing. "You give me credit for a strong will, then?"

"Yes," I said. "For a dangerously strong one."

"Why dangerous?" she asked in a tone of surprise.

"I think," I answered, "that any will which can exercise such power is dangerous — for there is always a chance of its being turned to bad uses."

"You would make me out a very dreadful individual, Mr Armitage," she said; and then looking up suddenly in my face — "You have never liked me. You are suspicious of me and distrust me, though I have never given you cause."

The accusation was so sudden and so true that I was unable to find any reply to it. She paused for a moment, and then said in a voice which was hard and cold:

"Don't let your prejudice lead you to interfere with me, however, or say anything to your friend Mr Cowles which might lead to a difference between us. You would find that to be a very bad policy."

There was something in the way she spoke which gave an indescribable air of a threat to these few words.

"I have no power," I said, "to interfere with your plans for the future. I cannot help, however, from what I have seen and heard, having fears for my friend."

"Fears!" she repeated, scornfully. "Pray, what have you seen and heard? Something from Mr Reeves, perhaps — I believe he is another of your friends?"

"He never mentioned your name to me," I answered truthfully enough. "You will be sorry to hear that he is dying." As I said it, we passed by a lighted window, and I glanced down to see what effect my words had upon her. She was laughing — there was no doubt of it; she was laughing quietly to herself. I could see merriment in every feature of her face. I feared and mistrusted the woman from that moment more than ever.

We said little more that night. When we parted, she gave me a quick, warning glance, as if to remind me of what she had said about the danger of interference. Her cautions would have made little difference to me could I have seen my way to benefiting Barrington Cowles by anything which I might say. But what could I say? I might say that her former suitors had been unfortunate. I might say that I believed her to be a cruel-hearted woman. I might say that I considered her to possess wonderful and almost preternatural powers. What impression would any of these accusations make upon an ardent lover — a man with my friend's enthusiastic temperament? I felt that it would be useless to advance them, so I was silent.

And now I come to the beginning of the end. Hitherto much has been surmise and inference and hearsay. It is my painful task to relate now, as dispassionately and as accurately as I can, what actually occurred under my own notice, and to reduce to writing the events which preceded the death of my friend.

Toward the end of the winter Cowles remarked to me that he intended to marry Miss Northcott as soon as possible — probably some time in the spring. He was, as I have already remarked, fairly well off, and the young lady had some money of her own, so that there was no pecuniary reason for a long engagement. "We are going to take a little house out at Corstorphine," he said, "and we hope to see your face at our table, Bob, as often as you can possibly come." I thanked him, and tried to shake off my apprehensions, and persuade myself that all would yet be well.

It was about three weeks before the time fixed for the marriage that Cowles remarked to me one evening that he feared he would be late that night. "I have had a note from Kate," he said, "asking me to call about eleven o'clock tonight, which seems rather a late hour, but perhaps she wants to talk over something quietly after old Mrs Merton retires."

It was not until after my friend's departure that I suddenly recollected the mysterious interview which I had been told of as preceding the suicide of young Prescott. Then I thought of the ravings of poor Reeves, rendered more tragic by the fact that I had heard that very day of his death. What was the meaning of it all? Had this woman some baleful secret to disclose which must be known before her marriage? Was it some reason which forbid her to marry? Or was it some reason which forbid others to marry her? I felt so uneasy that I would have followed Cowles, even at the risk of offending him, and endeavoured to dissuade him from keeping his appointment, but a glance at the clock showed me that I was too late. I was determined to wait up for his return, so I piled some coals upon the fire and took down a novel from the shelf. My thoughts proved more interesting than the book, however, and I threw it on one side. An indefinable feeling of anxiety and depression weighed upon me. Twelve o'clock came, and then half-past, without any sign of my friend. It was nearly one when I heard a step in the street outside, and then a knocking at the door. I was surprised, as I knew that my friend always carried a key — however, I hurried down and undid the latch. As the door flew open, I knew in a moment that my worst apprehensions had been fulfilled. Barrington Cowles was leaning against the railings outside, with his face sunk upon his breast, and his whole attitude expressive of the most intense despondency. As he passed in he gave a stagger, and would have fallen had I not thrown my left arm around him. Supporting him with this, and holding the lamp in my other hand, I led him slowly upstairs into our sitting-room. He sunk down upon the sofa without a word. Now that I could get a good view of him, I was horrified to see the change which had come over him. His face was deathly pale, and his very lips were bloodless. His cheeks and forehead were clammy, his eyes glazed, and his whole expression altered. He looked like a man who had gone through some terrible ordeal, and was thoroughly unnerved.

"My dear fellow, what is the matter?" I asked, breaking the silence. "Nothing amiss, I trust? Are you unwell?"

"Brandy!" he fairly gasped. "Give me some brandy!"

I took out the decanter, and was about to help him, when he snatched it from me with a trembling hand, and poured out nearly half a tumbler of the spirit. He was usually a most abstemious man, but he took this off at a gulp without adding any water to it. It seemed to do him good, for the colour began to come back to his face, and he leaned upon his elbow.

"My engagement is off, Bob," he said, trying to speak calmly, but with a tremor in his voice which he could not conceal. "It is all over."

"Cheer up!" I answered, trying to encourage him. "Don't get down on your luck. How was it? What was it all about?"

"About?" he groaned, covering his face with his hands. "If I did tell you, Bob, you would not believe it. It is too dreadful — too horrible — unutterably awful and incredible! Oh, Kate, Kate!" and he rocked himself to and fro in his grief; "I pictured you an angel and I find you a —"

"A what?" I asked, for he had paused.

He looked at me with a vacant stare, and then suddenly burst out, waving his arms: "A fiend!" he cried. "A ghoul from the pit! A vampire soul behind a lovely face! Now, God forgive me!" he went on in a lower tone, turning his face to the wall; "I have said more than I should. I have loved her too much to speak of her as she is. I love her too much now."

He lay still for some time, and I had hoped that the brandy had had the effect of sending him to sleep, when he suddenly turned his face toward me.

"Did you ever read of wehr-wolves?" he asked.

I answered that I had.

"There is a story," he said, thoughtfully, "in one of Marryat's books about a beautiful woman who took the form of a wolf at night and devoured her own children. I wonder what put that idea into Marryat's head?"

He pondered for some minutes, and then he cried out for some more brandy. There was a small bottle of laudanum upon the table, and I managed, by insisting upon helping him myself, to mix about half a dram with the spirits. He drank it off, and sunk his head once more upon the pillow. "Anything better than that," he groaned. "Death is better than that. Crime and cruelty; cruelty and crime. Anything is better than that;" and so on, with the monotonous refrain, until at last the words became indistinct, his eyelids closed over his weary eyes, and he sunk into a profound slumber. I carried him into his bedroom without arousing him; and making a couch for myself out of the chairs, I remained by his side all night.

In the morning Barrington Cowles was in a high fever. For weeks he lingered between life and death. The highest medical skill of Edinburgh was called in, and his vigorous constitution slowly got the better of his disease. I nursed him during this anxious time; but through all his wild delirium and ravings he never let a word escape him which explained the mystery connected with Miss Northcott. Sometimes he spoke of her in the tenderest words and most loving voice. At others he screamed out that she was a fiend, and stretched out his arms, as if to keep her off. Several times he cried that he would not sell his soul for a beautiful face, and then he would moan in a most piteous voice, "But I love her — I love her for all that; I shall never cease to love her."

When he came to himself he was an altered man. His severe illness had emaciated him greatly, but his dark eyes had lost none of their brightness. They shone out with startling brilliancy from under his dark, overhanging brows. His manner was eccentric and variable — sometimes irritable, sometimes recklessly mirthful, but never natural. He would glance about him in a strange, suspicious manner, like one who feared something, and yet hardly knew what it was he dreaded. He never mentioned Miss Northcott's name — never until that fatal evening of which I have now to speak.

In an endeavour to break the current of his thoughts by frequent change of scene, I travelled with him through the highlands of Scotland, and afterward down the east coast. In one of these peregrinations of ours we visited the Isle of May, an island near the mouth of the Firth of Forth, which, except in the tourist season, is singularly barren and desolate. Beyond the keeper of the lighthouse there are only one or two families of poor fisher-folk, who sustain a precarious existence by their nets, and by the capture of cormorants and solan geese. This grim spot seemed to have such a fascination for

Cowles that we engaged a room in one of the fishermen's huts, with the intention of passing a week or two there. I found it very dull, but the loneliness appeared to be a relief to my friend's mind. He lost the look of apprehension which had become habitual to him, and became something like his old self. He would wander round the island all day, looking down from the summit of the great cliffs which girt it round, and watching the long green waves as they came booming in and burst in a shower of spray over the rocks beneath.

One night — I think it was our third or fourth on the island — Barrington Cowles and I went outside the cottage before retiring to rest, to enjoy a little fresh air, for our room was small, and the rough lamp caused an unpleasant odour. How well I remember every little circumstance in connection with that night! It promised to be tempestuous, for the clouds were piling up in the northwest, and the dark wrack was drifting across the face of the moon, throwing alternate belts of light and shade upon the rugged surface of the island and the restless sea beyond.

We were standing talking close by the door of the cottage, and I was thinking to myself that my friend was more cheerful than he had been since his illness, when he gave a sudden, sharp cry, and looking round at him I saw, by the light of the moon, an expression of unutterable horror come over his features. His eyes became fixed and staring, as if riveted upon some approaching object, and he extended his long thin forefinger, which quivered as he pointed.

"Look there!" he cried. "It is she! It is she! You see her there coming down the side of the brae." He gripped me convulsively by the wrist as he spoke. "There she is, coming toward us!"

"Who?" I cried, straining my eyes into the darkness.

"She — Kate — Kate Northcott!" he screamed. "She has come for me! Hold me fast, old friend! Don't let me go!"

"Hold up, old man," I said, clapping him on the shoulder. "Pull yourself together; you are dreaming; there is nothing to fear."

"She is gone!" he cried, with a gasp of relief. "No, by Heaven! there she is again, and nearer — coming nearer! She told me she would come for me, and she keeps her word!"

"Come into the house," I said. His hand, as I grasped it, was as cold as ice.

"Ah, I knew it!" he shouted. "There she is, waving her arms. She is beckoning to me. It is the signal. I must go. I am coming, Kate; I am coming!"

THE
UNIVERSITY OF WINNIPEG
PORTAGE & BALMORAL
WINNIPEG, MAN.   R3B 2E9
CANADA

I threw my arms around him, but he burst from me with superhuman strength, and dashed into the darkness of the night. I followed him, calling to him to stop, but he ran the more swiftly. When the moon shone out between the clouds I could catch a glimpse of his dark figure, running rapidly in a straight line, as if to reach some definite goal. It may have been imagination, but it seemed to me that in the flickering light I could distinguish a vague something in front of him — a shimmering form which eluded his grasp and led him onward. I saw his outlines stand out hard against the sky behind him as he surmounted the brow of a little hill, then he disappeared, and that was the last ever seen by mortal eye of Barrington Cowles.

The fishermen and I walked round the island all that night with lanterns, and examined every nook and corner without seeing a trace of my poor lost friend. The direction in which he had been running terminated in a rugged line of jagged cliffs overhanging the sea. At one place here the edge was somewhat crumbled, and there appeared marks upon the turf which might have been left by human feet. We lay upon our faces at this spot, and peered with our lanterns over the edge, looking down on the boiling surge two hundred feet below. As we lay there, suddenly above the beating of the waves and the howling of the wind, there rose a strange, wild screech from the abyss below. The fishermen — a naturally superstitious race — averred that it was the sound of woman's laughter, and I could hardly persuade them to continue the search. For my own part I think it may have been the cry of some sea-fowl startled from its nest by the flash of the lantern. However that may be, I never wish to hear such a sound again.

And now I have come to the end of the painful duty which I have undertaken. I have told as plainly and as accurately as I could the story of the death of John Barrington Cowles, and the train of events which preceded it. I am aware that to others the sad episode seemed commonplace enough. Here is the prosaic account which appeared in *The Scotsman* a couple of days afterward:

"*Sad Occurrence on the Isle of May.*—The Isle of May has been the scene of a sad disaster. Mr John Barrington Cowles, a gentleman well known in University circles as a most distinguished student, and the present holder of the Neil Arnott prize for physics, has been recruiting his health in this quiet retreat. The night before last he suddenly left his friend, Mr Robert Armitage, and he has not since

39

been heard of. It is almost certain that he has met his death by falling over the cliffs which surround the island. Mr Cowles' health has been failing for some time, partly from overstudy and partly from worry connected with family affairs. By his death the University loses one of her most promising alumni."

I have nothing more to add to my statement. I have unburdened my mind of all that I know. I can well conceive that many, after weighing all that I have said, will see no ground for an accusation against Miss Northcott. They will say that, because a man of a naturally excitable disposition says and does wild things, and even eventually commits self-murder after a sudden and heavy disappointment, there is no reason why vague charges should be advanced against a young lady. To this I answer that they are welcome to their opinion. For my own part, I ascribe the death of William Prescott, of Archibald Reeves, and of John Barrington Cowles to this woman with as much confidence as if I had seen her drive a dagger into their hearts.

You ask me, no doubt, what my own theory is which will explain all these strange facts. I have none, or, at best, a dim and vague one. That Miss Northcott possessed extraordinary power over the minds, and through the minds over the bodies, of others, I am convinced, as well as that her instincts were to use this power for base and cruel purposes. That some even more fiendish and terrible phase of character lay behind this — some horrible trait which it was necessary for her to reveal before marriage — is to be inferred from the experience of her three lovers, while the dreadful nature of the mystery thus revealed can only be surmised from the fact that the very mention of it drove from her those who have loved her so passionately. Their subsequent fate was, in my opinion, the result of her vindictive remembrance of their desertion of her, and that they were forewarned of it at the time was shown by the words of both Reeves and Cowles. Above this, I can say nothing. I lay the facts soberly before the public as they came under my notice. I have never seen Miss Northcott since, nor do I wish to do so. If by the words I have written I can save any one human being from the snare of those bright eyes and that beautiful face, then I can lay down my pen with the assurance that my poor friend has not died altogether in vain.

THE PARASITE

MARCH 24th.—The spring is fairly with us now. Outside my laboratory window the great chestnut-tree is all covered with the big glutinous gummy buds, some of which have already begun to break into little green shuttlecocks. As you walk down the lanes you are conscious of the rich silent forces of nature working all around you. The wet earth smells fruitful and luscious. Green shoots are peeping out everywhere. The twigs are stiff with their sap; and the moist, heavy English air is laden with a faintly resinous perfume. Buds in the hedges, lambs beneath them — everywhere the work of reproduction going forward!

I can see it without and I can feel it within. We also have our spring when the little arterioles dilate, the lymph flows in a brisker stream, the glands work harder, winnowing and straining. Every year Nature readjusts the whole machine. I can feel the ferment in my blood at this very moment, and as the cool sunshine pours through my window I could dance about in it like a gnat. So I should, only that Charles Sadler would rush upstairs to know what was the matter. Besides, I must remember that I am Professor Gilroy. An old professor may afford to be natural, but when fortune has given one of the first chairs in the university to a man of four-and-thirty he must try and act the part consistently.

What a fellow Wilson is! If I could only throw the same enthusiasm into physiology that he does into psychology I should become a Claude Bernard at the least. His whole life and soul and energy work to one end. He drops to sleep collating his results of the past day, and he wakes to plan his researches for the coming one. And yet, outside the narrow circle who follow his proceedings he gets so little credit for it. Physiology is a recognised science. If I add even a brick to the edifice every one sees and applauds it. But Wilson is trying to dig the foundations for a science of the future. His work is underground and does not show. Yet he goes on uncomplainingly, corresponding with a hundred semi-maniacs in the hope of finding one reliable witness, sifting a hundred lies on the chance of gaining one little speck of truth, collating old books, devouring new ones, experimenting, lecturing, trying to light up in others the fiery interest which is consuming him. I am filled with wonder and admiration when I think of him; and yet, when he asks me to associate myself with his researches I am compelled to tell him that in their present state they offer little attraction to a man who is devoted to exact science. If he could show me something positive and objective, I might then be tempted to approach the question from its physiological side. So long as half his subjects are tainted with charlatanry and the other half with hysteria, we physiologists must content ourselves with the body and leave the mind to our descendants.

No doubt I am a materialist. Agatha says that I am a rank one. I tell her that is an excellent reason for shortening our engagement, since I am in such urgent need of her spirituality. And yet I may claim to be a curious example of the effect of education upon temperament, for by nature I am, unless I deceive myself, a highly psychic man. I was a nervous, sensitive boy, a dreamer, a somnambulist, full of impressions and intuitions. My black hair, my dark eyes, my thin olive face, my tapering fingers are all characteristic of my real temperament, and cause experts like Wilson to claim me as their own. But my brain is soaked with exact knowledge. I have trained myself to deal only with fact and with proof. Surmise and fancy have no place in my scheme of thought. Show me what I can see with my microscope, cut with my scalpel, weigh in my balance, and I will devote a lifetime to its investigation. But when you ask me to study feelings, impressions, suggestions, you ask me to do what is distasteful and even demoralising. A departure from pure reason affects me like an evil smell or a musical discord.

Which is a very sufficient reason why I am a little loth to go to Professor Wilson's tonight. Still, I feel that I could hardly get out of the invitation without positive rudeness — and now that Mrs Marden and Agatha are going, of course I would not if I could. But I had rather meet them anywhere else. I know that Wilson would draw me into this nebulous semi-science of his if he could. In his enthusiasm he is perfectly impervious to hints or remonstrances. Nothing short of a positive quarrel will make him realise my aversion to the whole business. I have no doubt that he has some new mesmerist, or clairvoyant, or medium, or trickster of some sort whom he is going to exhibit to us, for even his entertainments bear upon his hobby. Well, it will be a treat for Agatha at any rate. She is interested in it, as woman usually is in whatever is vague and mystical and indefinite.

10.50 p.m.—This diary-keeping of mine is, I fancy, the outcome of that scientific habit of mind about which I wrote this morning. I like to register impressions while they are fresh. Once a day at least I endeavour to define my own mental position. It is a useful piece of self-analysis, and has, I fancy, a steadying effect upon the character. Frankly, I must confess that my own needs what stiffening I can give it. I fear that after all much of my neurotic temperament survives, and that I am far from that cool, calm precision which characterises Murdoch or Pratt-Haldane. Otherwise, why should the tomfoolery which I have witnessed this evening have set my nerves thrilling so that even now I am all unstrung. My only comfort is that neither Wilson, nor Miss Penelosa, nor even Agatha could have possibly known my weakness.

And what in the world was there to excite me? Nothing, or so little that it will seem ludicrous when I set it down.

The Mardens got to Wilson's before me. In fact I was one of the last to arrive, and found the room crowded. I had hardly time to say a word to Mrs Marden and to Agatha, who was looking charming in white and pink with glittering wheat-ears in hair, when Wilson came twitching at my sleeve.

"You want something positive, Gilroy," said he, drawing me apart into a corner. "My dear fellow, I have a phenomenon — a phenomenon."

I should have been more impressed had I not heard the same before. His sanguine spirit turns every firefly into a star.

"No possible question about the bona fides this time," said he, in answer perhaps to some little gleam of amusement in my eyes. "My wife has known her for many years. They both come from Trinidad, you know. Miss Penelosa has only been in England a month or two, and knows no one outside the university circle; but I assure you that the things she has told us suffice in themselves to establish clairvoyance upon an absolutely scientific basis. There is nothing like her, amateur or professional. Come and be introduced!"

I like none of these mystery-mongers, but the amateur least of all. With the paid performer you may pounce upon him and expose him the instant that you have seen through his trick. He is there to deceive you, and you are there to find him out. But what are you to do with the friend of your host's wife? Are you to turn on a light suddenly and expose her slapping a surreptitious banjo? Or are you to hurl cochineal over her evening frock when she steals round with her phosphorous bottle and her supernatural platitude. There would be a scene, and you would be looked upon as a brute. So you have your choice of being that or a dupe. I was in no very good humour as I followed Wilson to the lady.

Anyone less like my idea of a West Indian could not be imagined. She was a small, frail creature, well over forty, I should say, with a pale, peaky face, and hair of a very light shade of chestnut. Her presence was insignificant and her manner retiring. In any group of ten women she would have been the last whom one would have picked out. Her eyes were perhaps her most remarkable, and also, I am compelled to say, her least pleasant feature. They were grey in colour — grey with a shade of green — and their expression struck me as being decidedly furtive. I wonder if furtive is the word, or should I have said fierce? On second thoughts, feline would have expressed it better. A crutch leaning against the wall told me, what was painfully evident when she rose, that one of her legs was crippled.

So I was introduced to Miss Penelosa, and it did not escape me that as my name was mentioned she glanced across at Agatha. Wilson had evidently been talking. And presently no doubt, thought I, she will inform me by occult means that I am engaged to a young lady with wheat-ears in her hair. I wondered how much more Wilson had been telling her about me.

"Professor Gilroy is a terrible sceptic," said he; "I hope, Miss Penelosa, that you will be able to convert him."

She looked keenly up at me.

"Professor Gilroy is quite right to be sceptical if he has not seen anything convincing," said she. "I should have thought," she added, "that you would yourself have been an excellent subject."

"For what, may I ask?" said I.

"Well, for mesmerism, for example."

"My experience has been, that mesmerists go for their subjects to those who are mentally unsound. All their results are vitiated, as it seems to me, by the fact that they are dealing with abnormal organisms."

"Which of these ladies would you say possessed a normal organism?" she asked. "I should like you to select the one who seems to you to have the best-balanced mind. Should we say the girl in pink

44

and white — Miss Agatha Marden, I think the name is?"

"Yes, I should attach weight to any results from her."

"I have never tried how far she is impressionable. Of course some people respond much more rapidly than others. May I ask how far your scepticism extends? I suppose that you admit the mesmeric sleep and the power of suggestion."

"I admit nothing, Miss Penelosa."

"Dear me, I thought science had got further than that. Of course I know nothing about the scientific side of it. I only know what I can do. You see the girl in red, for example, over near the Japanese jar. I shall will that she come across to us."

She bent forward as she spoke and dropped her fan upon the floor. The girl whisked round and came straight towards us, with an inquiring look upon her face as if someone had called her.

"What do you think of that, Gilroy?" cried Wilson in a kind of ecstasy.

I did not dare to tell him what I thought of it. To me it was the most barefaced, shameless piece of imposture that I had ever witnessed. The collusion and the signal had really been too obvious.

"Professor Gilroy is not satisfied," said she, glancing up at me with her strange little eyes. "My poor fan is to get the credit of that experiment. Well, we must try something else. Miss Marden, would you have any objection to my putting you off?"

"Oh, I should love it!" cried Agatha.

By this time all the company had gathered round us in a circle, the shirt-fronted men and the white-throated women, some awed, some critical, as though it were something between a religious ceremony and a conjurer's entertainment. A red velvet armchair had been pushed into the centre, and Agatha lay back in it, a little flushed and trembling slightly from excitement. I could see it from the vibration of the wheat-ears. Miss Penelosa rose from her seat and stood over her, leaning upon her crutch.

And there was a change in the woman. She no longer seemed small or insignificant. Twenty years were gone from her age. Her eyes were shining, a tinge of colour had come into her sallow cheeks, her whole figure had expanded. So I have seen a dull-eyed, listless lad change in an instant into briskness and life when given a task of which he felt himself master. She looked down at Agatha with an expression which I resented from the bottom of my soul — the expression with which a Roman empress might have looked at her kneeling slave. Then, with a quick commanding gesture, she tossed up her arms and swept them slowly down in front of her.

I was watching Agatha narrowly. During three passes she seemed to be simply amused. At the fourth I observed a slight glazing of her eyes, accompanied by some dilation of her pupils. At the sixth there was a momentary rigor. At the seventh her lids began to droop. At the tenth her eyes were closed, and her breathing was slower and fuller than usual. I tried as I watched to preserve my scientific calm, but a foolish, causeless agitation convulsed me. I trust that I hid it, but I felt as a child feels in the dark. I could not have believed that I was still open to such weakness.

"She is in the trance," said Miss Penelosa.

"She is sleeping," I cried.

"Wake her, then!"

I pulled her by the arm and shouted in her ear. She might have been dead for all the impression that I could make. Her body was there on the velvet chair. Her organs were acting, her heart, her lungs. But her soul! It had slipped from beyond our ken. Whither had it gone? What power had dispossessed it? I was puzzled and disconcerted.

"So much for the mesmeric sleep," said Miss Penelosa. "As regards suggestion, whatever I may suggest Miss Marden will infallibly do, whether it be now or after she has awakened from her trance. Do you demand proof of it?"

"Certainly," said I.

"You shall have it."

I saw a smile pass over her face as though an amusing thought had struck her. She stopped and whispered earnestly into her subject's ear. Agatha, who had been so deaf to me, nodded her head as she listened.

"Awake!" cried Miss Penelosa, with a sharp tap of her crutch upon the floor. The eyes opened, the glazing cleared slowly away, and the soul looked out once more after its strange eclipse.

We went away early. Agatha was none the worse for her strange excursion, but I was nervous and unstrung, unable to listen to or answer the stream of comments which Wilson was pouring out for my benefit. As I bade her goodnight, Miss Penelosa slipped a piece of paper into my hand.

"Pray forgive me," said she, "if I take means to overcome your scepticism. Open this note at ten o'clock tomorrow morning. It is a little private test."

I can't imagine what she means, but there is the note, and it shall be opened as she directs. My head is aching, and I have written enough for tonight. Tomorrow I dare say that what seems so inexplicable will take quite another complexion. I shall not surrender my convictions without a struggle.

March 25th.—I am amazed—confounded. It is clear that I must reconsider my opinion upon this matter. But first, let me place on record what has occurred.

I had finished breakfast and was looking over some diagrams with which my lecture is to be illustrated when my housekeeper entered to tell me that Agatha was in my study, and wished to see me immediately. I glanced at the clock, and saw with surprise that it was only half-past nine.

When I entered the room she was standing on the hearthrug facing me. Something in her pose chilled me, and checked the words which were rising to my lips. Her veil was half down, but I could see that she was pale, and that her expression was constrained.

"Austin," she said, "I have come to tell you that our engagement is at an end."

I staggered. I believe that I literally did stagger. I know that I found myself leaning against the bookcase for support.

"But — but —" I stammered, "this is very sudden, Agatha."

"Yes, Austin, I have come here to tell you that our engagement is at an end."

"But surely," I cried, "you will give me some reason. This is unlike you, Agatha. Tell me how I have been unfortunate enough to offend you."

"It is all over, Austin."

"But why? You must be under some delusion, Agatha. Perhaps you have been told some falsehood about me. Or you may have misunderstood something that I have said to you. Only let me know what it is, and a word may set it all right."

"We must consider it all at an end."

"But you left me last night without a hint at any disagreement. What could have occurred in the interval to change you so? It must have been something that happened last night. You have been thinking it over, and you have disapproved of my conduct. Was it the mesmerism? Did you blame me for letting that woman exercise her power over you? You know that at the least sign I should have interfered."

47

"It is useless, Austin. All is over." Her voice was cold and measured; her manner strangely formal and hard. It seemed to me that she was absolutely resolved not to be drawn into any argument or explanation. As for me, I was shaking with agitation, and I turned my face aside, so ashamed was I that she should see my want of control.

"You must know what this means to me," I cried. "It is the blasting of all my hopes and the ruin of my life. You surely will not inflict such a punishment upon me unheard. You will let me know what is the matter. Consider how impossible it would be for me, under any circumstances, to treat you so. For God's sake, Agatha, let me know what I have done."

She walked past me without a word and opened the door.

"It is quite useless, Austin," said she. "You must consider our engagement at an end." An instant later she was gone, and before I could recover myself sufficiently to follow her I heard the hall-door close behind her.

I rushed into my room to change my coat, with the idea of hurrying round to Mrs Marden's to learn from her what the cause of my misfortune might be. So shaken was I that I could hardly lace my boots. Never shall I forget those horrible ten minutes.

I had just pulled on my overcoat when the clock upon the mantelpiece struck ten.

Ten! I associated the idea with Miss Penelosa's note. It was lying before me on the table, and I tore it open. It was scribbled in pencil in a peculiarly angular handwriting.

"My dear Professor Gilroy," it said, "pray excuse the personal nature of the test which I am giving you. Professor Wilson happened to mention the relations between you and my subject of this evening, and it struck me that nothing could be more convincing to you than if I were to suggest to Miss Marden that she should call upon you at half-past nine tomorrow morning and suspend your engagement for half an hour or so. Science is so exacting that it is difficult to give a satisfying test, but I am convinced that this, at least, will be an action which she would be most unlikely to do of her own free-will. Forget anything that she may have said, as she has really nothing whatever to do with it, and will certainly not recollect anything about it. I write this note to shorten your anxiety, and to beg you to forgive me for the momentary unhappiness which my suggestion must have caused you.—Yours faithfully, Helen Penelosa."

Really when I had read the note I was too relieved to be angry. It was a liberty. Certainly it was a very great liberty indeed on the part of a lady whom I had only met once. But after all I had challenged her by my scepticism. It may have been, as she said, a little difficult to devise a test which would satisfy me.

And she had done that. There could be no question at all upon the point. For me hypnotic suggestion was finally established. It took its place from now onwards as one of the facts of life. That Agatha, who of all women of my acquaintance has the best-balanced mind, had been reduced to a condition of automatism appeared to be certain. A person at a distance had worked her as an engineer on the shore might guide a Brennan torpedo. A second soul had slipped in, as it were, had pushed her own aside, and had seized her nervous mechanism, saying, "I will work this for half an hour." And Agatha must have been unconscious as she came and as she returned. Could she make her way in safety through the streets in such a state! I put on my hat and hurried round to see if all was well with her.

Yes. She was at home. I was shown into the drawing-room, and found her sitting with a book upon her lap.

"You are an early visitor, Austin," said she, smiling.

"And you have been an even earlier one," I answered.

She looked puzzled. "What do you mean?" she asked.

"You have not been out today?"

"No, certainly not."

"Agatha," said I seriously. "Would you mind telling me exactly what you have done this morning?"

She laughed at my earnestness.

"You've got on your professorial look, Austin. See what comes of being engaged to a man of science. However, I will tell you, though I can't imagine what you want to know for. I got up at eight. I breakfasted at half-past. I came into this room at ten minutes past nine and began to read *The Memoirs of Madame de Rémusat*. In a few minutes I did the French lady the bad compliment of dropping to sleep over her pages, and I did you, sir, the very flattering one of dreaming about you. It is only a few minutes since I woke up."

"And found yourself where you had been before?"

"Why, where else should I find myself?"

"Would you mind telling me, Agatha, what it was that you dreamed about me? It really is not mere curiosity on my part."

"I merely had a vague impression that you came into it. I cannot recall anything definite."

"If you have not been out today, Agatha, how is it that your shoes are dusty?"

A pained look came over her face.

"Really, Austin, I do not know what is the matter with you this morning. One would almost think that you doubted my word. If my boots are dusty, it must be, of course, that I have put on a pair which the maid had not cleaned."

It was perfectly evident that she knew nothing whatever about the matter, and I reflected that after all perhaps it was better that I should not enlighten her. It might frighten her, and could serve no purpose that I could see. I said no more about it, therefore, and left shortly afterwards to give my lecture.

But I am immensely impressed. My horizon of scientific possibilities has suddenly been enormously extended. I no longer wonder at Wilson's demoniac energy and enthusiasm. Who would not work hard who had a vast virgin field ready to his hand? Why, I have known the novel shape of a nucleolus, or a trifling peculiarity of striped muscular fibre seen under a 300-diametre lens fill me with exultation. How petty do such researches seem when compared with this one which strikes at the very roots of life, and the nature of the soul! I had always looked upon spirit as a product of matter. The brain, I thought, secreted the mind, as the liver does the bile. But how can this be when I see mind working from a distance, and playing upon matter as a musician might upon a violin. The body does not give rise to the soul then, but is rather the rough instrument by which the spirit manifests itself. The windmill does not give rise to the wind, but only indicates it. It was opposed to my whole habit of thought, and yet it was undeniably possible and worthy of investigation.

And why should I not investigate it? I see that under yesterday's date I said, "If I could see something positive and objective I might be tempted to approach it from the physiological aspect." Well, I have got my test. I shall be as good as my word. The investigation would, I am sure, be of immense interest. Some of my colleagues might look askance at it, for science is full of unreasoning prejudices, but if Wilson has the courage of his convictions, I can afford to have it also. I shall go to him tomorrow morning — to him and to Miss Penelosa. If she can show us so much it is probable that she can show us more.

March 26th.—Wilson was, as I had anticipated, very exultant over my conversion, and Miss Penelosa was also demurely pleased at the result of her experiment. Strange what a silent colourless creature she is, save only when she exercises her power! Even talking about it gives her colour and life. She seems to take a singular interest in me. I cannot help observing how her eyes follow me about the room.

We had the most interesting conversation about her own powers. It is just as well to put her views on record, though they cannot of course claim any scientific weight.

"You are on the very fringe of the subject," said she, when I had expressed wonder at the remarkable instance of suggestion which she had shown me. "I had no direct influence upon Miss Marden when she came round to you. I was not even thinking of her that morning. What I did was to set her mind as I might set the alarum of a clock so that at the hour named it would go off of its own accord. If six months instead of twelve hours had been suggested, it would have been the same."

"And if the suggestion had been to assassinate me?"

"She would most inevitably have done so."

"But this is a terrible power!" I cried.

"It is, as you say, a terrible power," she answered gravely. "And the more you know of it the more terrible will it seem to you."

"May I ask," said I, "what you meant when you said that this matter of suggestion is only at the fringe of it? What do you consider the essential?"

"I had rather not tell you."

I was surprised at the decision of her answer.

"You understand," said I, "that it is not out of curiosity I ask, but in the hope that I may find some scientific explanation for the facts with which you furnish me."

"Frankly, Professor Gilroy," said she, "I am not at all interested in science, nor do I care whether it can or cannot classify these powers."

"But I was hoping ——"

"Ah, that is quite another thing. If you make it a personal matter," said she, with the pleasantest of smiles, "I shall be only too happy to tell you anything you wish to know. Let me see! What was it you asked me? Oh, about the further powers. Professor Wilson won't believe in them, but they are quite true all the same. For example, it is possible for an operator to gain complete command over his subject — presuming that the latter is a good one. Without any previous suggestion he may make him do whatever he likes."

"Without the subject's knowledge?"

"That depends. If the force were strongly exerted he would know no more about it than Miss Marden did when she came round and frightened you so. Or, if the influence were less powerful, he might be conscious of what he was doing but be quite unable to prevent himself from doing it."

"Would he have lost his own willpower, then?"

"It would be overridden by another, stronger one."

"Have you ever exercised this power yourself?"

"Several times."

"Is your own will so strong, then?"

"Well, it does not entirely depend upon that. Many have strong wills which are not detachable from themselves. The thing is to have the gift of projecting it into another person and superseding their own. I find that the power varies with my own strength and health."

"Practically, you send your soul into another person's body."

"Well, you might put it that way."

"And what does your own body do?"

"It merely feels lethargic."

"Well, but is there no danger to your own health?" I asked.

"There might be a little. You have to be careful never to let your own consciousness absolutely go, otherwise you might experience some difficulty in finding your way back again. You must always preserve the connection, as it were. I am afraid I express myself very badly, Professor Gilroy, but of course I don't know how to put these things in a scientific way. I am just giving you my own experiences and my own explanations."

Well, I read this over now at my leisure, and I marvel at myself! Is this Austin Gilroy, the man who has won his way to the front by his hard reasoning power and by his devotion to fact? Here I am gravely retailing the gossip of a woman, who tells me how her soul may be projected from her body, and how, while she lies in a lethargy, she can control the actions of people at a distance! Do I accept it? Certainly not. She must prove and re-prove before I yield a point. But if I am still a sceptic I have at least ceased to be a scoffer. We are to have a sitting this evening and she is to try if she can produce any mesmeric effect upon me. If she can it will make an excellent starting-point for our investigation. No one can accuse me, at any rate, of complicity. If she cannot, we must try and find some subject who will be like Caesar's wife. Wilson is perfectly impervious.

10 p.m.—I believe that I am on the threshold of an epoch-making investigation. To have the power of examining these phenomena from inside — to have an organism which will respond, and, at the same time, a brain which will appreciate and criticise — that is surely a unique advantage. I am quite sure that Wilson would give five years of his life to be as susceptible as I have proved myself to be.

There was no one present except Wilson and his wife. I was seated with my head leaning back, and Miss Penelosa, standing in front and a little way to the left, used the same long sweeping strokes as with Agatha. At each of them a warm current of air seemed to strike me and to suffuse a thrill and glow all through me from head to foot. My eyes were fixed upon Miss Penelosa's face, but as I gazed the features seemed to blur and to fade away. I was conscious only of her own eyes looking down at me, grey, deep, inscrutable. Larger they grew and larger, until they changed suddenly into two mountain lakes towards which I seemed to be falling with horrible rapidity. I shuddered, and as I did so some deeper stratum of thought told me that the shudder represented the rigor which I had observed in Agatha. An instant later I struck the surface of the lakes, now joined into one, and down I went beneath the water with a fulness in my head and a buzzing in my ears. Down I went, down, down, and then with a swoop up again until I could see the light streaming brightly through the green water. I was almost at the surface when the word "Awake!" rang through my head, and with a start I found myself back in the armchair, with Miss Penelosa leaning on her crutch, and Wilson, his notebook in his hand, peeping over her shoulder. No heaviness or weariness was left behind. On the contrary, though it is only an hour or so since the experiment, I feel so wakeful that I am more inclined for my study than my bedroom. I see quite a vista of interesting experiments extending before us, and am all impatience to begin upon them.

March 27th.—A blank day, as Miss Penelosa goes with Wilson and his wife to the Suttons. Have begun Binet and Ferré's *Animal Magnetism*. What strange, deep waters these are! Results, results, results — and the cause an absolute mystery. It is stimulating to the imagination, but I must be on my guard against that. Let us have no inferences nor deductions, and nothing but solid facts. I know that the mesmeric trance is true, I know that mesmeric suggestion is true, I know that I am myself sensitive to this force. That is my present position. I have a large new notebook, which shall be devoted entirely to scientific detail.

Long talk with Agatha and Mrs Marden in the evening about our marriage. We think that the summer vac. (the beginning of it) would be the best time for the wedding. Why should we delay? I grudge even those few months. Still, as Mrs Marden says, there are a good many things to be arranged.

March 28.—Mesmerised again by Miss Penelosa. Experience much the same as before, save that insensibility came on more quickly. See Notebook A for temperature of room, barometric pressure, pulse and respiration, as taken by Professor Wilson.

March 29.—Mesmerised again. Details in Notebook A.

March 30.—Sunday, and a blank day. I grudge any interruption of our experiments. At present they merely embrace the physical signs which go with slight, with complete, and with extreme insensibility. Afterwards we hope to pass on to the phenomena of suggestion and of lucidity. Professors have demonstrated these things upon women at Nancy, and at the Saltpetrière. It will be more convincing when a woman demonstrates it upon a professor, with a second professor as a witness. And that I should be the subject, I the sceptic, the materialist! At least I have shown that my devotion to science is greater than to my own personal consistency. The eating of our own words is the greatest sacrifice which truth ever requires of us.

My neighbour, Charles Sadler, the handsome young demonstrator of Anatomy, came in this evening to return a volume of Virchow's Archives which I had lent him. I call him young, but, as a matter of fact, he is a year older than I am.

"I understand, Gilroy," said he, "that you are being experimented upon by Miss Penelosa."

"Well," he went on, when I had acknowledged it, "if I were you I should not let it go any further. You will think me very impertinent, no doubt, but none the less I feel it to be my duty to advise you to have no more to do with her."

Of course I asked him why.

"I am so placed that I cannot enter into particulars as freely as I could wish," said he. "Miss Penelosa is the friend of my friend, and my position is a delicate one. I can only say this, that I have myself been the subject of some of the woman's experiments, and that they have left a most unpleasant impression upon my mind."

He could hardly expect me to be satisfied with that, and I tried hard to get something more definite out of him, but without success. Is it conceivable that he could be jealous at my having superseded him! Or is he one of those men of science who feel personally injured when facts run counter to their preconceived opinions? He cannot seriously suppose that because he has some vague grievance I am therefore to abandon a series of experiments which promise to be so fruitful of results. He appeared to be annoyed at the light way in which I treated his shadowy warnings, and we parted with some little coldness on both sides.

March 31st.—Mesmerised by Miss P.

April 1st.—Mesmerised by Miss P. (Notebook A).

April 2nd.—Mesmerised by Miss P. (Sphygmographic chart taken by Professor Wilson.)

April 3rd.—It is possible that this course of mesmerism may be a little trying to the general constitution. Agatha says that I am thinner, and darker under the eyes. I am conscious of a nervous irritability which I had not observed in myself before. The least noise, for example, makes me start, and the stupidity of a student causes me exasperation instead of amusement. Agatha wishes me to stop; but I tell her that every course of study is trying, and that one can never attain a result without paying some price for it. When she sees the sensation which my forthcoming paper on *The Relation between Mind and Matter* may make, she will understand that it is worth a little nervous wear-and-tear. I should not be surprised if I got my F.R.S. over it.

Mesmerised again in the evening. The effect is produced more rapidly now, and the subjective visions are less marked. I keep full notes of each sitting. Wilson is leaving for town for a week or ten days, but we shall not interrupt the experiments, which depend for their value as much upon my sensations as on his observations.

April 4th.—I must be carefully on my guard. A complication has crept into our experiments which I had not reckoned upon. In my eagerness for scientific facts I have been foolishly blind to the human relations between Miss Penelosa and myself. I can write here what I would not breathe to a living soul. The unhappy woman appears to have formed an attachment for me.

I should not say such a thing even in the privacy of my own intimate journal if it had not come to such a pass that it is impossible to ignore it. For some time — that is, for the last week — there have been signs, which I have brushed aside and refused to think of. Her brightness when I come, her dejection when I go, her eagerness that I should come often, the expression of her eyes, the tone of her voice. I tried to think that they meant nothing and were perhaps only her ardent West Indian manner. But last night as I woke from the mesmeric sleep I put out my hand, unconsciously, involuntarily, and clasped hers. When I came fully to myself we were sitting with them locked, she looked up at me with an expectant smile. And the horrible thing was that I felt impelled to say what she expected me to say. What a false wretch I should have been! How I should have loathed myself today had I yielded to the temptation of that moment! But, thank God, I was strong enough to spring up and to hurry from the room. I was rude, I fear, but I could not — no, I could not trust myself another moment. I, a gentleman, a man of honour, engaged to one of the sweetest girls in England — and yet in a moment of reasonless passion I nearly professed love for this woman whom I hardly know! She is far older than myself, and a cripple. It is monstrous — odious, — and yet the impulse was so strong that had I stayed another minute in her presence I should have committed myself. What was it? I have to teach others the workings of our organism, and what do I know of it myself! Was it the sudden up-cropping of some lower stratum in my nature — a brutal primitive instinct suddenly asserting itself? I could almost believe the tales of obsession by evil spirits, so overmastering was the feeling.

Well, the incident places me in a most unfortunate position. On the one hand, I am very loth to abandon a series of experiments which have already gone so far, and which promise such brilliant results. On the other, if this unhappy woman has conceived a passion for me — but surely even now I must have made some hideous mistake. She, with her age and her deformity. It is impossible. And then she knew about Agatha. She understood how I was placed. She only smiled out of amusement, perhaps, when in my dazed state I seized her hand. It was my half-mesmerised brain which gave it a meaning, and sprang with such bestial swiftness to meet it. I wish I could persuade myself that it was indeed so. On the whole, perhaps, my wisest plan would be to postpone our other experiments until Wilson's return. I have written a note to Miss Penelosa, therefore, making no allusion to last night, but saying that a press of work would cause me to interrupt our sittings for a few days. She has answered, formally enough, to say that if I should change my mind I should find her at home at the usual hour.

10 p.m.—Well, well, what a thing of straw I am! I am coming to know myself better of late, and the more I know the lower I fall in my own estimation. Surely I was not always so weak as this. At four o'clock I should have smiled had anyone told me that I should go to Miss Penelosa's tonight; and yet at eight I was at Wilson's door as usual. I don't know how it occurred. The influence of habit, I suppose. Perhaps there is a mesmeric craze as there is an opium craze, and I am a victim to it. I only know that as I worked in my study I became more and more uneasy. I fidgeted. I worried. I could not concentrate my mind upon the papers in front of me. And then, at last, almost before I knew what I was doing, I seized my hat and hurried round to keep my usual appointment.

We had an interesting evening. Mrs Wilson was present during most of the time, which prevented the embarrassment which one at least of us must have felt. Miss Penelosa's manner was quite the same as usual, and she expressed no surprise at my having come in spite of my note. There was nothing in her bearing to show that yesterday's incident had made any impression upon her, and so I am inclined to hope that I overrated it.

April 6th (evening).—No, no, I did not overrate it. I can no longer attempt to conceal from myself that this woman has conceived a passion for me. It is monstrous, but it is true. Again, tonight, I awoke from the mesmeric trance to find my hand in hers, and to suffer that odious feeling which urges me to throw away my honour, my career — everything — for the sake of this creature who, as I can plainly see when I am away from her influence, possesses no single charm upon earth. But when I am near her I do not feel this. She rouses something in me — something evil — something I had rather not think of. She paralyses my better nature, too, at the moment when she stimulates my worse. Decidedly it is not good for me to be near her.

Last night was worse than before. Instead of flying I actually sat for some time with my hand in hers, talking over the most intimate subjects with her. We spoke of Agatha among other things. What could I have been dreaming of! Miss Penelosa said that she was conventional, and I agreed with her. She spoke once or twice in a disparaging way of her, and I did not protest. What a creature I have been!

Weak as I have proved myself to be, I am still strong enough to bring this sort of thing to an end. It shall not happen again. I have sense enough to fly when I cannot fight. From this Sunday night onwards I shall never sit with Miss Penelosa again. Never! Let the experiments go, let the research come to an end, anything is better than facing this monstrous temptation which drags me so low. I have said nothing to Miss Penelosa, but I shall simply stay away. She can tell the reason without any words of mine.

April 7th.—Have stayed away as I said. It is a pity to ruin such an interesting investigation, but it would be a greater pity still to ruin my life, and I know that I cannot trust myself with that woman.

11 p.m.—God help me! What is the matter with me! Am I going mad? Let me try and be calm and reason with myself. First of all I shall set down exactly what occurred.

It was nearly eight when I wrote the lines with which this day begins. Feeling strangely restless and uneasy, I left my rooms and walked round to spend the evening with Agatha and her mother. They both remarked that I was pale and haggard. About nine Professor Pratt-Haldane came in, and we played a game of whist. I tried hard to concentrate my attention upon the cards, but the feeling of restlessness grew and grew until I found it impossible to struggle against it. I simply could not sit still at the table. At last, in the very middle of a hand, I threw my cards down, and, with some sort of an incoherent apology about having an appointment, I rushed from the room. As if in a dream, I have a vague recollection of tearing through the hall, snatching my hat from the stand, and slamming the door behind me. As in a dream, too, I have the impression of the double line of gas-lamps, and my bespattered boots tell me that I must have run down the middle of the road. It was all misty and strange and unnatural. I came to Wilson's house, I saw Mrs Wilson and I saw Miss Penelosa. I hardly recall what we talked about, but I do remember that Miss Penelosa shook the head of her crutch at me in a playful way, and accused me of being late and of losing interest in our experiments. There was no mesmerism, but I stayed some time and have only just returned.

My brain is quite clear again, now, and I can think over what has occurred. It is absurd to suppose that it is merely weakness and force of habit. I tried to explain it in that way the other night, but it will no longer suffice. It is something much deeper and more terrible than that. Why, when I was at the Mardens' whist-table I was dragged away, as if the noose of a rope had been cast round me. I can no longer disguise it from myself. The woman has her grip upon me. I am in her clutch. But I must keep my head and reason it out, and see what is best to be done.

But what a blind fool I have been! In my enthusiasm over my research I have walked straight into the pit, although it lay gaping before me. Did she not herself warn me? Did she not tell me, as I can read in my own journal, that when she has acquired power over a subject she can make him do her will? And she has acquired that power over me. I am, for the moment, at the beck and call of this creature with the crutch. I must come when she wills it. I must do as she wills. Worst of all, I must feel as she wills. I loathe her and fear her, yet while I am under the spell she can doubtless make me love her.

There is some consolation in the thought, then, that these odious impulses for which I have blamed myself do not really come from me at all. They are all transferred from her, little as I could have guessed it at the time. I feel cleaner and lighter for the thought.

April 8th.—Yes, now in broad daylight, writing coolly and with time for reflection, I am compelled to confirm everything which I find in my journal last night. I am in a horrible position, but, above all, I must not lose my head. I must pit my intellect against her powers. After all, I am no silly puppet to dance at the end of a string. I have energy, brains, courage. For all her devil's tricks I may beat her yet. May! I must, or what is to become of me?

Let me try to reason it out. This woman, by her own explanation, can dominate my nervous organism. She can project herself into my body and take command of it. She has a parasitic soul — yes, she is a parasite, a monstrous parasite. She creeps into my frame as the hermit crab does into the whelk's shell. I am powerless! What can I do? I am dealing with forces of which I know nothing. And I can tell no one of my trouble. They would set me down as a madman.

Certainly, if it got noised abroad, the university would say that they had no need of a devil-ridden professor. And Agatha! No, no, I must face it alone.

I read over my notes of what the woman said when she spoke about her powers. There is one point which fills me with dismay. She implies that when the influence is slight the subject knows what he is doing but cannot control himself, whereas, when it is strongly exerted, he is absolutely unconscious. Now, I have always known what I did, though less so last night than on the previous occasion. That seems to mean that she has never yet exerted her full powers upon me. Was ever a man so placed before! Yes, perhaps there was, and very near me too. Charles Sadler must know something of this! His vague words of warning take a meaning now. Oh, if I had only listened to him then, before I helped by those repeated sittings to forge the links of the chain which binds me. But I will see him today. I will apologise to him for having treated his warning so lightly. I will see if he can advise me.

4 p.m.—No, he cannot. I have talked with him, and he showed such surprise at the first words in which I tried to express my unspeakable secret that I went no further. As far as I can gather (by hints and inferences rather than by any statement), his own experience was limited to some words or looks such as I have myself endured. His abandonment of Miss Penelosa is in itself a sign that he was never really in her toils. Oh, if he only knew his escape! He has to thank his phlegmatic Saxon temperament for it. I am black and Celtic, and this hag's clutch is deep in my nerves. Shall I ever get it out? Shall I ever be the same man that I was just one short fortnight ago?

Let me consider what I had better do. I cannot leave the university in the middle of the term. If I were free my course would be obvious. I should start at once and travel in Persia. But would she allow me to start? And could her influence not reach me in Persia, and bring me back to within touch of her crutch? I can only find out the limits of this hellish power by my own bitter experience. I will fight and fight and fight — and what can I do more?

I know very well that about eight o'clock tonight that craving for her society — that irresistible restlessness — will come upon me. How shall I overcome it? What shall I do? I must make it impossible for me to leave the room. I shall lock the door and throw the key out of the window. But then, what am I to do in the morning? Never mind about the morning. I must at all costs break this chain which holds me.

April 9.—Victory! I have done splendidly! At seven o'clock last night I took a hasty dinner and then locked myself up in my bedroom and dropped the key into the garden. I chose a cheery novel, and lay in bed for three hours trying to read it, but really in a horrible state of trepidation, expecting every instant that I should become conscious of the impulse. Nothing of the sort occurred, however, and I awoke this morning with the feeling that a black nightmare had been lifted off me. Perhaps the creature realised what I had done, and understood that it was useless to try to influence me. At any rate, I have beaten her once, and if I can do it once I can do it again.

It was most awkward about the key in the morning. Luckily there was an under-gardener below, and I asked him to throw it up. No doubt he thought I had just dropped it. I will have doors and windows screwed up and six stout men to hold me down in my bed before I will surrender myself to be hag-ridden in this way. I had a note from Mrs Marden this afternoon asking me to go round and see her. I intended to do so in any case, but had not expected to find bad news waiting for me. It seems that the Armstrongs, from whom Agatha has expectations, are due home from Adelaide in the *Aurora*, and that they have written to Mrs Marden and her to meet them in town. They will probably be away for a month or six weeks, and as the *Aurora* is due on Wednesday they must go at once — tomorrow if they are ready in time. My consolation is that when we meet again there will be no more parting between Agatha and me.

"I want you to do one thing, Agatha," said I, when we were alone together. "If you should happen to meet Miss Penelosa, either in town or here, you must promise me never again to allow her to mesmerise you."

Agatha opened her eyes.

"Why it was only the other day that you were saying how interesting it all was, and how determined you were to finish your experiments."

"I know, but I have changed my mind since then."

"And you won't have it anymore?"

"No."

"I am so glad, Austin. You can't think how pale and worn you have been lately. It was really our principal objection to going to London now, that we did not wish to leave you when you were so pulled down. And your manner has been so strange occasionally — especially that night when you left poor Professor Pratt-Haldane to play dummy. I am convinced that these experiments are very bad for your nerves."

"I think so too, dear."

"And for Miss Penelosa's nerves as well. You have heard that she is ill?"

"No."

"Mrs Wilson told us so last night. She described it as a nervous fever. Professor Wilson is coming back this week, and of course Mrs Wilson is very anxious that Miss Penelosa should be well again then, for he has quite a programme of experiments which he is anxious to carry out."

I was glad to have Agatha's promise, for it was enough that this woman should have one of us in her clutch. On the other hand, I was disturbed to hear about Miss Penelosa's illness. It rather discounts the victory which I appeared to win last night. I remember that she said that loss of health interfered with her power. That may be why I was able to hold my own so easily. Well, well, I must take the same precautions tonight and see what comes of it. I am childishly frightened when I think of her.

April 10.—All went very well last night. I was amused at the gardener's face when I had again to hail him this morning and to ask him to throw up my key. I shall get a name among the servants if this sort of thing goes on. But the great point is that I stayed in my room without the slightest inclination to leave it. I do believe that I am shaking myself clear of this incredible bond — or is it only that the woman's power is in abeyance until she recovers her strength. I can but pray for the best.

The Mardens left this morning, and the brightness seems to have gone out of the spring sunshine. And yet it is very beautiful also as it gleams on the green chestnuts opposite my windows, and gives a touch of gaiety to the heavy lichen-mottled walls of the old colleges. How sweet and gentle and soothing is Nature! Who would think that there lurked in her also such vile forces, such odious possibilities! For of course I understand that this dreadful thing which has sprung out at me is neither supernatural nor even preternatural. No, it is a natural force which this woman can use and society is ignorant of. The mere fact that it ebbs with her strength shows how entirely it is subject to physical laws. If I had time I might probe it to the bottom and lay my hands upon its antidote. But you cannot tame the tiger when you are beneath his claws. You can but try to writhe away from him. Ah, when I look in the glass and see my own dark eyes and clear-cut Spanish face I long for a vitriol splash or a bout of the small-pox. One or the other might have saved me from this calamity.

I am inclined to think that I may have trouble tonight. There are two things which make me fear so. One is, that I met Mrs Wilson on the street and that she tells me that Miss Penelosa is better, though still weak. I find myself wishing in my heart that the illness had been her last. The other is, that Professor Wilson comes back in a day or two, and his presence would act as a constraint upon her. I should not fear our interviews, if a third person were present. For both these reasons I have a presentiment of trouble tonight, and I shall take the same precautions as before.

April 10.—No, thank God, all went well last night. I really could not face the gardener again. I locked my door and thrust the key underneath it, so that I had to ask the maid to let me out in the morning. But the precaution was really not needed, for I never had any inclination to go out at all. Three evenings in succession at home! I am surely near the end of my troubles, for Wilson will be home again either today or tomorrow. Shall I tell him of what I have gone through or not? I am convinced that I should not have the slightest sympathy from him. He would look upon me as an interesting case, and read a paper about me at the next meeting of the Psychical Society, in which he would gravely discuss the possibility of my being a deliberate liar, and weigh it against the chances of my being in an early stage of lunacy. No, I shall get no comfort out of Wilson.

I am feeling wonderfully fit and well. I don't think I ever lectured with greater spirit. Oh, if I could only get this shadow off my life how happy I should be! Young, fairly wealthy, in the front rank of my profession, engaged to a beautiful and charming girl — have I not everything which a man could ask for? Only one thing to trouble me, but what a thing it is!

Midnight.—I shall go mad. Yes, that will be the end of it. I shall go mad. I am not far from it now. My head throbs as I rest it on my hot hand. I am quivering all over like a scared horse. Oh, what a night I have had! And yet I have some cause to be satisfied also.

At the risk of becoming the laughing-stock of my own servant I again slipped my key under the door, imprisoning myself for the night. Then, finding it too early to go to bed, I lay down with my clothes on and began to read one of Dumas' novels. Suddenly I was gripped — gripped and dragged from the couch. It is only thus that I can describe the overpowering nature of the force which pounced upon me. I clawed at the coverlet. I clung to the woodwork. I believe that I screamed out in my frenzy. It was all useless — hopeless. I must go. There was no way out of it. It was only at the outset that I resisted. The force soon became too overmastering for that. I thank goodness that there were no watchers there to interfere with me. I could not have answered for myself if there had been. And besides the determination to get out, there came to me also the keenest and coolest judgment in choosing my means. I lit a candle and endeavoured, kneeling in front of the door, to pull the key through with the feather-end of a quill pen. It was just too short and pushed it further away. Then with quiet persistence I got a paper-knife out of one of the drawers, and with that I managed to draw the key back. I opened the door, stepped into my study, took a photograph of myself from the bureau, wrote something across it, placed it in the inside pocket of my coat, and then started off for Wilson's.

It was all wonderfully clear, and yet disassociated from the rest of my life, as the incidents of even the most vivid dream might be. A peculiar double consciousness possessed me. There was the predominant alien will, which was bent upon drawing me to the side of its owner, and there was the feebler protesting personality, which I recognised as being myself, tugging feebly at the overmastering impulse as a led terrier might at its chain. I can remember recognising these two conflicting forces, but I recall nothing of my walk, nor of how I was admitted to the house. Very vivid, however, is my recollection of how I met Miss Penelosa. She was reclining on the sofa in the little boudoir in which our experiments had usually been carried out. Her head was rested on her hand, and a tiger-skin rug had been partly drawn over her. She looked up expectantly as I entered, and, as the lamplight fell upon her face, I could see that she was very pale and thin, with dark hollows under her eyes. She smiled at me and pointed to a stool beside her. It was with her left hand that she pointed, and I, running eagerly forward, seized it — I loathe myself as I think of it — and pressed it passionately to my lips. Then, seating myself upon the stool, and still retaining her hand, I gave her the photograph which I had brought with me, and talked, and talked, and talked, of my love for her, of my grief over her illness, of my joy at her recovery, of the misery it was to me to be absent a single evening from her side. She lay quietly looking down at me with imperious eyes and her provocative smile. Once I remember that she passed her hand over my hair as one caresses a dog. And it gave me pleasure, the caress. I thrilled under it. I was her slave, body and soul, and for the moment I rejoiced in my slavery.

And then came the blessed change. Never tell me that there is not a Providence. I was on the brink of perdition. My feet were on the edge. Was it a coincidence that at that very instant help should come! No, no, no, there is a Providence, and His hand has drawn me back. There is something in the universe stronger than this devil woman with her tricks. Ah, what a balm to my heart it is to think so!

As I looked up at her I was conscious of a change in her. Her face, which had been pale before, was now ghastly. Her eyes were dull and the lids drooped heavily over them. Above all, the look of serene confidence had gone from her features. Her mouth had weakened. Her forehead had puckered. She was frightened and undecided. And, as I watched the change, my own spirit fluttered and struggled, trying hard to tear itself from the grip which held it — a grip which from moment to moment grew less secure.

"Austin," she whispered, "I have tried to do too much. I was not strong enough. I have not recovered yet from my illness. But I could not live longer without seeing you. You won't leave me, Austin. This is only a passing weakness. If you will only give me five minutes I shall be myself again. Give me the small decanter from the table in the window."

But I had regained my soul. With her waning strength the influence had cleared away from me and left me free. And I was aggressive — bitterly, fiercely aggressive. For once, at least, I could make this woman understand what my real feelings towards her were. My soul was filled with a hatred as bestial as the love against which it was a reaction. It was the savage, murderous passion of the revolted serf. I could have taken the crutch from her side and beaten her face in with it. She threw her hands up, as if to avoid a blow, and cowered away from me into the corner of the settee.

"The brandy!" she gasped. "The brandy!"

I took the decanter and poured it over the roots of a palm in the window. Then I snatched the photograph from her hand and tore it into a hundred pieces.

"You vile woman!" I said. "If I did my duty to society you would never leave the room alive."

"I love you, Austin. I love you," she wailed.

"Yes," I cried. "And Charles Sadler before. And how many others before that?"

"Charles Sadler!" she gasped. "He has spoken to you! So, Charles Sadler, Charles Sadler!" Her voice came through her white lips like a snake's hiss.

"Yes, I know you, and others shall know you too. You shameless creature! You knew how I stood. And yet you used your vile power to bring me to your side. You may perhaps do so again, but at least you will remember that you have heard me say that I love Miss Marden from the bottom of my soul, and that I loathe you, abhor you. The very sight of you and the sound of your voice fill me with horror and disgust. The thought of you is repulsive. That is how I feel towards you, and if it pleases you by your tricks to draw me again to your side, as you have done tonight, you will at least, I should think, have little satisfaction in trying to make a lover out of a man who has told you his real opinion of you. You may put what words you will into my mouth, but you cannot help remembering ——"

I stopped, for the woman's head had fallen back and she had fainted. She could not bear to hear what I had to say to her. What a glow of satisfaction it gives me to think that come what may in the future she can never misunderstand my true feelings towards her. But what will occur in the future? What will she do next? I dare not think of it. Oh, if only I could hope that she will leave me alone! But when I think of what I said to her — never mind, I have been stronger than she for once.

April 11.—I hardly slept last night, and found myself in the morning so unstrung and feverish that I was compelled to ask Pratt-Haldane to do my lecture for me. It is the first that I have ever missed. I rose at midday; but my head is aching, my hands quivering, and my nerves in a pitiable state.

Who should come round this evening but Wilson. He has just come back from London, where he has lectured, read papers, convened meetings, exposed a medium, conducted a series of experiments on thought transference, entertained Professor Richet of Paris, spent hours gazing into a crystal, and obtained some evidence as to the passage of matter through matter. All this he poured into my ears in a single gust.

"But you," he cried at last, "you are not looking well. And Miss Penelosa is quite prostrated today. How about the experiments?"

"I have abandoned them."

"Tut, tut! Why?"

"The subject seems to me to be a dangerous one."

Out came his big brown notebook.

"This is of great interest," said he. "What are your grounds for saying it is a dangerous one? Please give your facts in chronological order with approximate dates, and names of reliable witnesses with their permanent addresses."

"First of all," I asked, "would you tell me whether you have collected any cases where the mesmerist has gained a command over the subject and has used it for evil purposes?"

"Dozens," he cried exultantly. "Crime by suggestion ——"

"I don't mean suggestion. I mean where a sudden impulse comes from a person at a distance — an uncontrollable impulse."

"Obsession!" he shrieked, in an ecstasy of delight. "It is the rarest condition. We have eight cases, five well attested. You don't mean to say ——" his exultation made him hardly articulate.

"No, I don't," said I. "Good evening! You will excuse me, but I am not very well tonight." And so at last I got rid of him, still brandishing his pencil and his notebook. My troubles may be bad to bear, but at least it is better to hug them to myself than to have myself exhibited by Wilson, like a freak at a fair. He has lost sight of human beings. Everything to him is a case and a phenomenon. I will die before I speak to him again upon the matter.

April 12.—Yesterday was a blessed day of quiet, and I enjoyed an uneventful night. Wilson's presence is a great consolation. What can the woman do now? Surely when she has heard me say what I have said she will conceive the same disgust for me which I have for her. She could not — no, she could not — desire to have a lover who had insulted her so. No, I believe I am free from her love — but how about her hate? Might she not use these powers of hers for revenge? Tut, why should I frighten myself over shadows! She will forget about me and I shall forget about her, and all will be well.

April 13.—My nerves have quite recovered their tone. I really believe that I have conquered the creature. But I must confess to living in some suspense. She is well again, for I hear that she was driving with Mrs Wilson in the High Street in the afternoon.

April 14.—I do wish I could get away from the place altogether. I shall fly to Agatha's side the very day that the term closes. I suppose it is pitiably weak of me, but this woman gets upon my nerves most terribly. I have seen her again, and I have spoken with her.

It was just after lunch, and I was smoking a cigarette in my study when I heard the step of my servant Murray in the passage. I was languidly conscious that a second step was audible behind, and had hardly troubled myself to speculate who it might be, when suddenly a slight noise brought me out of my chair with my skin creeping with apprehension. I had never particularly observed before what sort of sound the tapping of a crutch was, but my quivering nerves told me that I heard it now in the sharp wooden clack which alternated with the muffled thud of the footfall. Another instant and my servant had shown her in.

I did not attempt the usual conventions of society, nor did she. I simply stood with the smouldering cigarette in my hand and gazed at her. She in her turn looked silently at me, and at her look I remembered how in these very pages I had tried to define the expression of her eyes, whether they were furtive or fierce. Today they were fierce — coldly and inexorably so.

"Well," said she at last, "are you still of the same mind as when I saw you last?"

"I have always been of the same mind."

"Let us understand each other, Professor Gilroy," said she slowly. "I am not a very safe person to trifle with, as you should realise by now. It was you who asked me to enter into a series of experiments with you, it was you who won my affections, it was you who professed your love for me, it was you who brought me your own photograph with words of affection upon it, and finally, it was you who on the very same evening thought fit to insult me most outrageously, addressing me as no man has ever dared to speak to me yet. Tell me that those words came from you in a moment of passion, and I am prepared to forget and to forgive them. You did not mean what you said, Austin? You do not really hate me?"

I might have pitied this deformed woman — such a longing for love broke suddenly through the menace of her eyes. But then I thought of what I had gone through, and my heart set like flint.

"If ever you heard me speak of love," said I, "you know very well that it was your voice which spoke and not mine. The only words of truth which I have ever been able to say to you are those which you heard when last we met."

"I know. Someone has set you against me. It was he." She tapped with her crutch upon the floor. "Well, you know very well that I could bring you this instant crouching like a spaniel to my feet. You will not find me again in my hours of weakness when you can insult me with impunity. Have a care what you are doing, Professor Gilroy. You stand in a terrible position. You have not yet realised the hold which I have upon you."

I shrugged my shoulders and turned away.

"Well," said she, after a pause, "if you despise my love I must see what can be done with fear. You smile, but the day will come when you will come screaming to me for pardon. Yes, you will grovel on the ground before me, proud as you are, and you will curse the day that ever you turned me from your best friend into your most bitter enemy. Have a care, Professor Gilroy." I saw a white hand shaking in the air, and a face which was scarcely human so convulsed was it with passion. An instant later she was gone, and I heard the quick hobble and tap receding down the passage.

But she has left a weight upon my heart. Vague presentiments of coming misfortune lie heavy upon me. I try in vain to persuade myself that these are only words of empty anger. I can remember those relentless eyes too clearly to think so. What shall I do — ah, what shall I do? I am no longer master of my own soul. At any moment this loathsome parasite may creep into me, and then ——? I must tell someone my hideous secret — I must tell it or go mad. If I had someone to sympathise and advise! Wilson is out of the question. Charles Sadler would understand me only so far as his own experience carries him. Pratt-Haldane! He is a well-balanced man, a man of great common sense and resource. I will go to him. I will tell him everything. God grant that he may be able to advise me!

6.45 p.m.—No, it is useless. There is no human help for me. I must fight this out singlehanded. Two courses lie before me: I might become the woman's lover, or I must endure such persecutions as she can inflict upon me. Even if none come I shall live in a hell of apprehension. But she may torture me, she may drive me mad, she may kill me, I will never, never, never give in. What can she inflict which would be worse than the loss of Agatha, and the knowledge that I am a perjured liar and have forfeited the name of gentleman?

Pratt-Haldane was most amiable, and listened with all politeness to my story. But when I looked at his heavy set features, his slow eyes, and the ponderous study furniture which surrounded him, I could hardly tell him what I had come to say. It was all so substantial, so material. And besides, what would I myself have said a short month ago if one of my colleagues had come to me with a story of demoniac possession? Perhaps I should have been less patient than he was. As it was, he took notes of my statement, asked me how much tea I drank, how many hours I slept, whether I had been overworking much, had I had sudden pains in the head, evil dreams, singing in the ears, flashes before the eyes — all questions which pointed to his belief that brain congestion was at the bottom of my trouble. Finally, he dismissed me with a great many platitudes about open-air exercise and avoidance of nervous excitement. His prescription, which was for chloral and bromide, I rolled up and threw into the gutter.

No, I can look for no help from any human being. If I consult any more they may put their heads together and I may find myself in an asylum. I can but grip my courage with both hands and pray that an honest man may not be abandoned.

April 15.—It is the sweetest spring within the memory of man. So green, so mild, so beautiful! Ah, what a contrast between Nature without and my own soul, so torn with doubt and terror! It has been an uneventful day, but I know that I am on the edge of an abyss. I know it, and yet I go on with the routine of my life. The one bright spot is that Agatha is happy and well, and out of all danger. If this creature had a hand on each of us, what might she not do?

April 16.—The woman is ingenious in her torments. She knows how fond I am of my work, and how highly my lectures are thought of. So it is from that point that she now attacks me. It will end, I can see, in my losing my professorship, but I will fight to the finish. She shall not drive me out of it without a struggle.

I was not conscious of any change during my lecture this morning, save that for a minute or two I had a dizziness and swimminess which rapidly passed away. On the contrary, I congratulated myself upon having made my subject (the functions of the red corpuscles) both interesting and clear. I was surprised, therefore, when a student came into my laboratory immediately after the lecture and complained of being puzzled by the discrepancy between my statements and those in the textbooks. He showed me his notebook, in which I was reported as having in one portion of the lecture championed the most outrageous and unscientific heresies. Of course I denied it, and declared that he had misunderstood me; but on comparing his notes with those of his companions, it became clear that he was right, and that I really had made some most preposterous statements. Of course I shall explain it away as being the result of a moment of aberration, but I feel only too sure that it will be the first of a series. It is but a month now to the end of the session, and I pray that I may be able to hold out until then.

April 26.—Ten days have elapsed since I have had the heart to make any entry in my journal. Why should I record my own humiliation and degradation! I had vowed never to open it again. And yet the force of habit is strong, and here I find myself taking up once more the record of my own dreadful experiences — in much the same spirit in which a suicide has been known to take notes of the effects of the poison which killed him.

Well, the crash which I had foreseen has come — and that no further back than yesterday. The university authorities have taken my lectureship from me. It has been done in the most delicate way, purporting to be a temporary measure to relieve me from the effects of overwork and to give me the opportunity of recovering my health. None the less it has been done, and I am no longer Professor Gilroy. The laboratory is still in my charge, but I have little doubt that that also will soon go.

The fact is that my lectures had become the laughing-stock of the university. My class was crowded with students who came to see and hear what the eccentric professor would do or say next. I cannot go into the detail of my humiliation. Oh, that devilish woman! There is no depth of buffoonery and imbecility to which she has not forced me. I would begin my lecture clearly and well — but always with the sense of a coming eclipse. Then as I felt the influence I would struggle against it, striving with clenched hands and beads of sweat upon my brow to get the better of it, while the students, hearing my incoherent words and watching my contortions, would roar with laughter at the antics of their professor. And then, when she had once fairly mastered me, out would come the most outrageous things: silly

71

jokes, sentiments as though I were proposing a toast, snatches of ballads, personal abuse even against some member of my class. And then in a moment my brain would clear again and my lecture proceed decorously to the end. No wonder that my conduct has been the talk of the colleges! No wonder that the university senate has been compelled to take official notice of such a scandal. Oh, that devilish woman!

And the most dreadful part of it all is my own loneliness. Here I sit in a commonplace English bow-window looking out upon a commonplace English street, with its garish 'busses and its lounging policemen, and behind me there hangs a shadow which is out of all keeping with the age and place. In the home of knowledge I am weighed down and tortured by a power of which science knows nothing. No magistrate would listen to me. No paper would discuss my case. No doctor would believe my symptoms. My own most intimate friends would only look upon it as a sign of brain derangement. I am out of all touch with my kind. Oh, that devilish woman! Let her have a care! She may push me too far. When the law cannot help a man he may make a law for himself.

She met me in the High Street yesterday evening and spoke to me. It was as well for her, perhaps, that it was not between the hedges of a lonely country road. She asked me with her cold smile whether I had been chastened yet. I did not deign to answer her. "We must try another turn of the screw," said she. Have a care, my lady, have a care! I had her at my mercy once. Perhaps another chance may come.

April 28.—The suspension of my lectureship has had the effect also of taking away her means of annoying me, and so I have enjoyed two blessed days of peace. After all, there is no reason to despair. Sympathy pours in to me from all sides, and everyone agrees that it is my devotion to science and the arduous nature of my researches which have shaken my nervous system. I have had the kindest message from the council, advising me to travel abroad, and expressing the confident hope that I may be able to resume all my duties by the beginning of the summer term. Nothing could be more flattering than their allusions to my career and to my services to the university. It is only in misfortune that one can test one's own popularity. This creature may weary of tormenting me, and then all may yet be well. May God grant it!

April 29.—Our sleepy little town has had a small sensation. The only knowledge of crime which we ever have is when a rowdy undergraduate breaks a few lamps, or comes to blows with a policeman. Last night, however, there was an attempt made to break into the branch of the Bank of England, and we are all in a flutter in consequence.

Parkinson the manager is an intimate friend of mine, and I found him very much excited when I walked round there after breakfast. Had the thieves broken into the counting-house they would still have had the safes to reckon with, so that the defence was considerably stronger than the attack. Indeed the latter does not appear to have ever been very formidable. Two of the lower windows have marks as if a chisel or some such instrument had been pushed under them to force them open. The police should have a good clue, for the woodwork had been done with green paint only the day before, and from the smears it is evident that some of it has found its way on to the criminal's hands or clothes.

4.30 p.m.—Ah, that accursed woman! That thrice-accursed woman! Never mind! She shall not beat me! No, she shall not! But oh, the she-devil! She has taken my professorship; now she would take my honour. Is there nothing I can do against her, nothing save — ah, but hard pushed as I am I cannot bring myself to think of that!

It was about an hour ago that I went into my bedroom and was brushing my hair before the glass when suddenly my eyes lit upon something which left me so sick and cold that I sat down upon the edge of the bed and began to cry. It is many a long year since I shed tears, but all my nerve was gone, and I could but sob and sob in impotent grief and anger. There was my house jacket, the coat I usually wear after dinner, hanging on its peg by the wardrobe, with the right sleeve thickly crusted from wrist to elbow with daubs of green paint.

So this was what she meant by another turn of the screw! She had made a public imbecile of me. Now she would brand me as a criminal. This time she has failed. But how about the next? I dare not think of it — and of Agatha, and my poor old mother! I wish that I were dead!

Yes, this is the other turn of the screw. And this is also what she meant, no doubt, when she said that I had not realised yet the power she has over me. I look back at my account of my conversation with her, and I see how she declared that with a slight exertion of her will her subject would be conscious, and with a stronger one unconscious.

Last night I was unconscious. I could have sworn that I slept soundly in my bed without so much as a dream. And yet those stains tell me that I dressed, made my way out, attempted to open the bank windows, and returned. Was I observed? Is it possible that someone saw me do it and followed me home! Ah, what a hell my life has become! I have no peace, no rest. But my patience is nearing its end.

10 p.m.—I have cleaned my coat with turpentine. I do not think that anyone could have seen me. It was with my screwdriver that I made the marks. I found it all crusted with paint, and I have cleaned it. My head aches as if it would burst, and I have taken five grains of antipyrene. If it were not for Agatha I should have taken fifty and had an end of it.

May 3.—Three quiet days. This hell-fiend is like a cat with a mouse. She lets me loose only to pounce upon me again. I am never so frightened as when everything is still. My physical state is deplorable — perpetual hiccough and ptosis of the left eyelid. I have heard from the Mardens that they will be back the day after tomorrow. I do not know whether I am glad or sorry. They were safe in London. Once here they may be drawn into the miserable network in which I am myself struggling. And I must tell them of it. I cannot marry Agatha so long as I know that I am not responsible for my own actions. Yes, I must tell them, even if it brings everything to an end between us.

Tonight is the university ball, and I must go. God knows I never felt less in the humour for festivity, but I must not have it said that I am unfit to appear in public. If I am seen there and have speech with some of the elders of the university it will go a long way towards showing them that it would be unjust to take my chair away from me.

11.30 p.m.—I have been to the ball. Charles Sadler and I went together, but I have come away before him. I shall wait up for him, however, for indeed I fear to go to sleep these nights. He is a cheery, practical fellow, and a chat with him will steady my nerves. On the whole, the evening was a great success. I talked to everyone who has influence, and I think that I made them realise that my chair is not vacant quite yet. The creature was at the ball — unable to dance, of course, but sitting with Mrs Wilson. Again and again her eyes rested upon me. They were almost the last things I saw before I left the room. Once as I sat sideways to her I watched her and saw that her gaze was following someone else. It was Sadler, who was dancing at the time with the second Miss Thurston. To judge by her expression it is well for him that he is not in her grip as I am. He does not know the escape he has had. I think I hear his step in the street now, and I will go down and let him in. If he will ——

May 4.—Why did I break off in this way last night? I never went downstairs after all — at least I have no recollection of doing so. But, on the other hand, I cannot remember going to bed. One of my hands is greatly swollen this morning, and yet I have no remembrance of injuring it yesterday. Otherwise I am feeling all the better for last night's festivity. But I cannot understand how it is that I did not meet Charles Sadler when I so fully intended to do so. Is it possible — my God, it is only too probable! Has she been leading me some devil's dance again? I will go down to Sadler and ask him.

Midday.—The thing has come to a crisis. My life is not worth living. But if I am to die then she shall come also. I will not leave her behind to drive some other man mad as she has me. No, I have come to the limit of my endurance. She has made me as desperate and dangerous a man as walks the earth. God knows I have never had the heart to hurt a fly, and yet if I had my hands now upon that woman she should never leave this room alive. I shall see her this very day, and she shall learn what she has to expect from me. I went to Sadler and found him to my surprise in bed. As I entered he sat up and turned a face towards me which sickened me as I looked at it.

"Why, Sadler, what has happened?" I cried, but my heart turned cold as I said it.

"Gilroy," he answered, mumbling with his swollen lips, "I have for some weeks been under the impression that you are a madman. Now I know it, and that you are a dangerous one as well. If it were not that I am unwilling to make a scandal in the college you would now be in the hands of the police."

"Do you mean ——?" I cried.

"I mean that as I opened the door last night you rushed out upon me, struck me with both your fists in the face, knocked me down, kicked me furiously on the side, and left me lying almost unconscious in the street. Look at your own hand bearing witness against you."

Yes, there it was, puffed up with sponge-like knuckles as after some terrific blow. What could I do? Though he put me down as a madman I must tell him all. I sat by his bed and went over all my troubles from the beginning. I poured them out with quivering hands and burning words which might have carried conviction to the most sceptical.

"She hates you and she hates me," I cried. "She revenged herself last night on both of us at once. She saw me leave the ball and she must have seen you also. She knew how long it would take you to reach home. Then she had but to use her wicked will. Ah, your bruised face is a small thing beside my bruised soul!"

He was struck by my story. That was evident. "Yes, yes, she watched me out of the room," he muttered. "She is capable of it. But is it possible that she has really reduced you to this? What do you intend to do?"

"To stop it," I cried. "I am perfectly desperate. I shall give her fair warning today, and the next time will be the last."

"Do nothing rash," said he.

"Rash!" I cried. "The only rash thing is that I should postpone it another hour." With that I rushed to my room. And here I am on the eve of what may be the great crisis of my life. I shall start at once. I have gained one thing today, for I have made one man at least realise the truth of this monstrous experience of mine. And, if the worst should happen, this diary remains as a proof of the goad that has driven me.

Evening.—When I came to Wilson's I was shown up, and found that he was sitting with Miss Penelosa. For half an hour I had to endure his fussy talk about his recent research into the exact nature of the spiritualistic rap, while the creature and I sat in silence looking across the room at each other. I read a sinister amusement in her eyes, and she must have seen hatred and menace in mine. I had almost despaired of having speech with her when he was called from the room and we were left for a few minutes together.

"Well, Professor Gilroy—or is it Mr Gilroy?" said she, with that bitter smile of hers, "how is your friend Mr Charles Sadler after the ball?"

"You fiend!" I cried, "you have come to the end of your tricks now. I will have no more of them. Listen to what I say." — I strode across and shook her roughly by the shoulder. "As sure as there is a God in heaven I swear that if you try another of your devilries upon me I will have your life for it. Come what may, I will have your life. I have come to the end of what a man can endure."

"Accounts are not quite settled between us," said she, with a passion that equalled my own. "I can love and I can hate. You had your choice. You chose to spurn the first, now you must test the other. It will take a little more to break your spirit, I see, but broken it shall be. Miss Marden comes back tomorrow as I understand."

"What has that to do with you?" I cried. "It is a pollution that you should dare even to think of her. If I thought that you would harm her ——"

She was frightened I could see, though she tried to brazen it out. She read the black thought in my mind and cowered away from me.

"She is fortunate in having such a champion," said she. "He actually dares to threaten a lonely woman. I must really congratulate Miss Marden upon her protector."

The words were bitter, but the voice and manner were more acid still.

"There is no use talking," said I. "I only came here to tell you — and to tell you most solemnly — that your next outrage upon me will be your last." With that, as I heard Wilson's step upon the stairs, I walked from the room. Ay, she may look venomous and deadly, but for all that she is beginning to see now that she has as much to fear from me as I can have from her. Murder! It has an ugly sound. But you don't talk of murdering a snake or of murdering a tiger. Let her have a care now.

May 5.—I met Agatha and her mother at the station at eleven o'clock. She is looking so bright, so happy, so beautiful. And she was so overjoyed to see me. What have I done to deserve such love! I went back home with them and we lunched together. All the troubles seem in a moment to have been shredded back from my life. She tells me that I am looking pale, and worried, and ill. The dear child puts it down to my loneliness and the perfunctory attentions of a housekeeper. I pray that she may never know the truth! May the shadow, if shadow there must be, lie ever black across my life and leave hers in the sunshine! I have just come back from them, feeling a new man. With her by my side I think that I could show a bold face to anything which life might send.

5 p.m.—Now let me try to be accurate. Let me try to say exactly how it occurred. It is fresh in my mind and I can set it down correctly, though it is not likely that the time will ever come when I shall forget the doings of today.

I had returned from the Mardens after lunch, and was cutting some microscopic sections in my freezing microtome, when in an instant I lost consciousness in the sudden hateful fashion which has become only too familiar to me of late.

When my senses came back to me I was sitting in a small chamber very different from the one in which I had been working. It was cosy and bright, with chintz-covered settees, coloured hangings, and a thousand pretty little trifles upon the wall. A small ornamental clock ticked in front of me, and the hands pointed to half-past three. It was all quite familiar to me, and yet I stared about for a moment in a half-dazed way until my eyes fell upon a cabinet photograph of myself upon the top of the piano. At the other side stood one of Mrs Marden. Then, of course, I remembered where I was. It was Agatha's boudoir.

But how came I there, and what did I want? A horrible sinking came to my heart. Had I been sent here on some devilish errand? Had that errand already been done? Surely it must, otherwise why should I be allowed to come back to consciousness. Oh, the agony of that moment! What had I done! I sprang to my feet in my despair, and as I did so a small glass bottle fell from my knees on to the carpet.

It was unbroken and I picked it up. Outside was written *Sulphuric Acid. Fort.* When I drew the round glass stopper a thick fume rose slowly up and a pungent choking smell pervaded the room. I recognised it as one which I kept for chemical testing in my chambers. But why had I brought a bottle of vitriol into Agatha's chamber? Was it not this thick reeking liquid with which jealous women had been known to mar the beauty of their rivals! My heart stood still as I held the bottle to the light. Thank God, it was full! No mischief had been done as yet. But had Agatha come in a minute sooner, was it not certain that the hellish parasite within me would have dashed the stuff on to her — ah! it will not bear to be thought of. But it must have been for that. Why else should I have brought it? At the thought of what I might have done my worn nerves broke down and I sat shivering and twitching, the pitiable wreck of a man. It was the sound of Agatha's voice and the rustle of her dress which restored me. I looked up and saw her blue eyes, so full of tenderness and pity, gazing down at me.

"We must take you away to the country, Austin," she said, "you want rest and quiet. You look wretchedly ill."

78

"Oh, it is nothing," said I, trying to smile. "It was only a momentary weakness. I am all right again now."

"I am so sorry to keep you waiting. Poor boy, you must have been here for quite half an hour. The vicar was in the drawing-room, and as I knew that you did not care for him I thought it better that Jane should show you up here. I thought the man would never go."

"Thank God he stayed! Thank God he stayed!" I cried hysterically.

"Why, what is the matter with you, Austin?" she asked, holding my arm as I staggered up from the chair. "Why are you glad that the vicar stayed? And what is this little bottle in your hand?"

"Nothing," I cried, thrusting it into my pocket. "But I must go. I have something important to do."

"How stern you look, Austin. I have never seen your face like that. You are angry?"

"Yes, I am angry."

"But not with me?"

"No, no, my darling. You would not understand."

"But you have not told me why you came."

"I came to ask you whether you would always love me — no matter what I did or what shadow might fall on my name. Would you believe in me and trust me however black appearances might be against me?"

"You know that I would, Austin."

"Yes, I know that you would. What I do I shall do for you. I am driven to it. There is no other way out, my darling!" I kissed her and rushed from the room.

The time for indecision was at an end. As long as the creature threatened my own prospects and my honour there might be a question as to what I should do. But now when Agatha — my innocent Agatha — was endangered, my duty lay before me like a turnpike-road. I had no weapon, but I never paused for that. What weapon should I need when I felt every muscle quivering with the strength of a frenzied man? I ran through the streets, so set upon what I had to do that I was only dimly conscious of the faces of friends whom I met — dimly conscious also that Professor Wilson met me, running with equal precipitance in the opposite direction. Breathless but resolute I reached the house and rang the bell. A white-cheeked maid opened the door, and turned whiter yet when she saw the face that looked in at her.

"Show me up at once to Miss Penelosa," I demanded.

"Sir," she gasped, "Miss Penelosa died this afternoon at half-past three."

AN ESSAY

UPON THE VASOMOTOR CHANGES
IN TABES DORSALIS AND ON THE
INFLUENCE WHICH IS EXERTED BY
THE SYMPATHETIC NERVOUS
SYSTEM IN THAT DISEASE, BEING A
THESIS PRESENTED IN THE HOPE OF
OBTAINING THE DEGREE OF
DOCTORSHIP OF MEDICINE OF THE
UNIVERSITY OF EDINBURGH.

by A. CONAN DOYLE, M.B., C.M.

It would be fair to say that "The Vasomotor Changes in Tabes Dorsalis" has never been among the most widely read works of Doyle. But it occupied an important place in the author's career, for it was the thesis that gained him the degree of M.D. – Doctor of Medicine – from Edinburgh University, in 1885. Like the majority of theses, it was destined to languish unpublished, and seldom consulted, on the shelves of the university library; but two extracts are of general interest and are reproduced above and below.

Tabes dorsalis is, in fact, a late complication of syphilis. The curious symptoms arise because the disease attacks the posterior columns of the spinal cord, and the posterior roots by which the nerve fibes enter the cord. This leads to loss of sensation, and to incoordination of the movements of the limbs, even though the strength of the muscles themselves remains unimpaired. The thesis argued that the disease causes spasm in the small arteries (the arterioles) supplying the spinal cord. Then those nerves which had the most precarious blood supply would be the first to be started of blood and perish. Fortunately, nowadays the question is academic because syphilis is easily cured by penicillin. Such serious, irreversible complications as tabes dorsalis are therefore exceptionally rare, although every medical student is still lectured on them ad nauseam.

It should be remembered that in Britain, unlike America, the M.D. is a postgraduate degree – the medical equivalent of a Ph.D. The first degree is the "bachelor of medicine" which is not a doctorate even though the holder is conventionally called "doctor". (But American students do not start medical school until they have completed a B.Sc., usually in rodent psychology.) An

M.D. of Edinburgh University has a certain scarcity value because it can only be conferred on those who acquired their first medical degree from Edinburgh, as Doyle had done in 1881. At the time of submitting his thesis he was practising as a G.P. in Southsea, by Portsmouth, not particularly successfully. In writing it he was seeking academic, not literary, repute. But there were times when he forgot this, and found himself writing a short story instead, as the first extract shows.

GRAHAM SUTTON

******

III. *The Clinical Symptoms of Tabes*

HAVING now discussed briefly the region of the human frame in which the effects of tabes are most visible in this region, and given a short summary of the various views put forward to account for the disease, it may be as well to run over the clinical symptoms visible in an ideal case of tabes.

The sufferer is commonly a man of between five-and-twenty and fifty. In many cases he is of that swarthy neurotic type which furnishes the world with an undue proportion of poets, musicians and madmen. In nine cases out of ten he has had syphilis, possibly a year ago, more probably four, eight, twelve or even twenty years before.

Eye symptoms are very commonly the first to drive the patient to seek medical advice. His wife calls his attention to the fact that he has developed a squint, or he finds a dimness come over his sight and the lines of his morning paper become blurred and blotted. Very commonly one of his eyelids drop and he finds he cannot raise it. His medical adviser on examining his eyesight finds that the visual angle is contracted, that scotomata or blurred patches occur in the circle of vision, and that the pupil which has perhaps been mydriatic is now myotic. Examination shows him also perhaps that this pupil while accommodating itself for distance, does not answer to the stimulus of light. Atropia may not cause it to dilate. An ophthalmoscopic examination may show atrophy of the optic nerve, the arteries being reduced in size and the disc grey and diminished.

There are no more constant symptoms in tabes than the pupillary ones. Vincent found them in 47 cases out of 51.

The patient returns home after this examination and may notice little or no change in his condition for years. Various little symptoms show him, however, that the demon which has seized him has not relaxed its grip. He may have fleeting attacks of facial neuralgia and even of facial paralysis. Strange flushes come over him and he perspires profusely without obvious cause. Numbness and pricklings alternate in different parts of his frame. His sexual desire, which has possibly for some time back been inordinate, begins to wane. Vague pains which have been flitting about his lower limbs and which he has probably ascribed to rheumatism, become more intense and sudden in their character until he can only compare them to electric shocks.

The sufferer's appetite has been probably capricious for some time back and his digestion uncertain. Suddenly some day after a meal he is seized by an irresistible attack of nausea. He vomits for hours, throwing up not only all that he has eaten but also many pints of a clear mucoid fluid, occasionally stained with blood or mixed with bile. The attack continues until he is utterly exhausted. This is a gastric crisis. Or it may be a violent attack of diarrhoea with tenesmus and innumerable watery stools. Or it may be a sudden cough with difficulty of breathing, simulating whooping cough and going to such a length that the sufferer becomes black in the face and may even expire of apnoea in the paroxysms. These latter are the intestinal and laryngeal crises.

For some time the friends of the patient have observed an uncertainty in his gait, which continues until walking becomes a matter of difficulty. He himself makes the discovery some night that without a light he is helpless, and falls to the ground. With this fresh budget of symptoms he seeks his medical man once more.

On examination the latter finds that the knee-jerk is gone, and possibly the cremasteric and gluteal reflexes as well. On being asked to shut his eyes the patient totters. There is no loss of muscular power, beyond that which is inevitable in a long illness.

After this, presuming the disease continues to run its course without check, the foregoing symptoms increase in severity while others gradually develop themselves. A feeling of constant constriction round the waist or under the armpits is a common phenomenon. Renal crises in which great quantities of pale urine of low specific gravity are passed, are rarer. The victim seldom escapes vescical troubles however, with cystitis and a constant desire to micturate, or the bladder may be sluggish so that there is no desire to micturate, or there may be vescical crises causing intolerable agony during many hours.

Occasionally stranger symptoms may come upon the sufferer. A small raw spot upon the plantar aspect of his foot may deepen and enlarge until a perforating ulcer is established. Or certain of his joints may become flooded by a sudden copious effusion, which rapidly bursts the ligaments, destroys the joint and causes atrophy of the articular ends of the bones. Or there may be changes in the shafts of the bones themselves by which they are rendered brittle and liable to fracture.

The skin during this time has been pallid, dry and cold, and subject to various eruptions, to herpes, pemphigus, erythema, and a condition resembling icthyosis.

As the disease progresses the sufferer gets some relief from pain, the sudden shocks dying away and being replaced by analgesia and anaesthesia. Motor paralysis and acute muscular atrophy may supervene. Slowly the unfortunate victim sinks from one gradation of misery to another and can only look forward to the death which may reach him from pure exhaustion or may come from the involvement of the vital centres in the medulla. Here are the words of Heine the great German Jewish poet when after seven years of this torture he saw the shades of death gather round his couch. They are interesting as showing the thoughts evolved by a great brain when linked to what was practically a dead body.

"Do I really exist?" he writes. "My body is so shrunken that I am hardly anything but a voice. In my mattress grave in the great city I hear early and late nothing but the noise of vehicles, hammering, quarrelling and piano-strumming. A grave without repose, death without the privileges of the dead who at least need not spend any money nor write letters or books — that is indeed a pitiful condition. Long ago the measure has been taken for my coffin and my obituary; but I die so slowly that the process is tedious for myself as well as my friends. What avails me that youths and maidens crown my marble bust with laurel when the withered hands of an aged hag are putting blisters behind my ears. What avails me the incense of the roses of Shiraz when in the wearisome loneliness of my sickroom I get no perfume but the smell of hot towels? But patience, everything has an end! You will one day find the booth closed where the puppet show of my humour has so often delighted you."

******

In the second extract Doyle suggested that it would be logical to treat the patient with a drug that dilates the small arteries, such as nitroglycerine. Ironically, today we have banished tabes only to replace it with an epidemic of heart disease, and nitroglycerine is nowadays used to dilate the coronary arteries of patients with angina. In the case described below, the ending, though not as unhappy as in the first extract, was not as satisfactory as a good novelist would wish. One wonders to what extent Doyle (or indeed any other medical author) was impelled into a literary career by the inherent cussedness of real-life people, and by a desire to replace them with fictional characters who could be guaranteed not to spoil the ending he had planned for them.

[G.C.S.]

It is no part of the object of this small thesis to go into the large and important subject of treatment. There is one note, however, which I should like to make. Presuming that the theory of the disease here advanced has any truth in it, the earliest condition of it is a general contraction of arterioles. Under these circumstances a drug which will dilate those vessels again ought to exert a favourable influence upon the disease. Of such drugs there are two which have a powerful action, nitrite of amyl and nitroglycerine. The former is a somewhat awkward drug to exhibit and its effect appears to be more transient than the other. Nitroglycerine, however, in a one per cent solution is a most handy and convenient preparation. The dose, beginning with one drop may be safely increased to fifteen or twenty, a congestive headache being the first sign of an overdose. I have myself taken as many as forty minims of Murrell's solution without inconvenience.

Only on one occasion have I been able to try this drug upon a tabid patient. Empiric experiments of the sort should only be tried with the knowledge and consent of the patient, and this makes it a delicate matter for a young practitioner. He is liable to fall a victim to the "post hoc propter hoc" fallacy, and all subsequent developments of the malady be laid to the door of that unfortunate innovation in the treatment. In this one case, however, the sufferer being an intelligent man, I proposed to him that he should try this remedy to which he readily consented. He had loss of reflexes, Brauch Romberg's symptom, amblyopia and every other sign of the malady. For two or three weeks he appeared to improve considerably both in his general health and in his particular symptoms. Though confined to a bathchair he pursued his avocation as a commercial traveller, and following this he passed on to another town, taking some of the drug with him. I have never heard from him since nor can I find out his address. It is such cases which tend to make medical men cynical. . . .

P6